S0-ARL-565

Needled to Death
by RL Beck

© RLBeck 2017 all rights reserved.
The characters and events in this book are fictitious. Any resemblance to real people, places, things and events is coincidental and not intended by the author.

Papa
as a dutiful daughter I listened
but the only way to get what you want
is to write your own.

Table of Contents

CHAPTER 1

Tessa blew in like a technicolor tornado closing the door behind her. She spun, wet drops of snow glistening on her eyelashes.

"Amy!" she cried, "boy, I'm glad to be out of that!" She waved at the door and the sleeting snow she'd left outside. I grinned, moving a little farther down the hall to watch as she began shedding her winter gear, every piece made by her clever hands. First, her 'tea cozy,' a large red tam with purple, yellow and smaller green pom-poms cascading down the side. "Catch!", she laughed lobbing it like a frisbee in my direction. I missed and it landed on the mat with a wet plop looking like a stranded sea creature. Smiling I picked it up. Next, she slid off her gloves, each finger a different color. They dangled from the wrists of her sweater coat, connected by a braided yarn rope through the sleeves. Then she slipped off the coat. I took it with care. While the color was not my favorite, a neon mustard, like splats left behind at hot dog stands, the coat itself was beautifully designed, it was a work of art. Last were her leggings. They too were a marvel of ingenuity and craftsmanship, a knitted combination of red leather strips and deep purple feather wool. Boots for a fairy I thought as I carefully hung the kaleidoscope of colors to dry.

By the time I finished she had slipped on gold plastic slippers. Whirling into my living room, she pulled out a little stool and sat with a thump. "Its foul out there! A perfect night for knitting up a storm," she grinned scanning the group. "I'm last again! How does that always happen," she asked, genuinely perplexed?

I smiled and slipped into my chair. It is no secret, Tessa is always late and she loves to make an entrance.

"This time I have a reason. A really good one," she said triumphantly.

"Okay, I'll bite," Jen said, "what's your excuse?" Jen tucked a strand of golden blonde hair behind her ear and sat forward expectantly.

"I saw the most gorgeous man on the street," Tessa announced with a gleam in her eye. "He's going from door to door and headed this way. I plan to answer the door, bat my eyes at him and find out what he wants." She giggled, "I'm hoping it's me." *6 + you = 7 so total = 9, NOT 8*

Amidst laughter, our neighborhood knit night began. Including Tessa, there were six women gathered in my tiny living room. It was rare for all of the *NINE* members to be present and tonight both Claire and Meg were out of town.

Minnie, our oldest member and Mariko, the Japanese exchange student who is living with her, sat side by side on the love seat under the window. Best friends, George and Jen were in each of the wing chairs, Tessa perched on the padded stool and I had my grandfather's rocker in the corner. In the centre of the room, an oversize ottoman serves as extra seating, storage, and my coffee table. It was warm and cozy and as Tessa said a perfect night for knitting.

George brought us back on topic as she always does. "Seeing a man on the street does not explain why you were late but I'll let that go for the moment," she paused, holding up her hand to stop Tessa's sputtering response. George is a litigator and has a flair for courtroom dramatics. "Gorgeous or not, why is this Adonis going from door to door? Is he selling something? Real Estate? Scout goodies? Insurance?"

Tessa was grinning, "I think not! And anyway he is a hunk. But, Counselor, I submit that he may be an officer of the law as there is a patrol car parked on the street."

There was a pause as the news sunk in then Minnie sagged in her seat as her knitting slid from her fingers and lay limply on her lap, the ball of yarn rolling to the floor. She gasped softly and murmured something. I thought I heard her say, "how?" but that didn't make sense. Jen recovered first, "Minnie, what's the matter? You're so pale." Mariko reached down to retrieve the wool and held it out, Minnie didn't notice, she hadn't moved. I sat forward and urged, "Minnie, please, you're scaring me! Are you ill?"

CONFUSED OR CONFUSEDLY?

Slowly she raised her eyes, "What? No. sorry," she said confusedly. She shook her head slightly as though to clear it, "I'm fine. I was thinking of something else but I'm fine." She sounded better, her voice stronger though she was still pale.

Jen opened her mouth to speak and closed it abruptly as we listened to heavy footsteps crunching up my icy stairs. Minnie took a deep breath and let it out slowly. The doorbell rang and Minnie looked at the group with a pained smile, "It's okay, honestly. I'm just tired."

Puzzled but relieved, I relaxed slightly. Answers to whatever had just happened would have to wait.

Tessa made her way to the door giving Minnie's knee a squeeze as she left the room. Minnie slowly picked up her knitting. She knits toques, scarves, and mittens for charity. She makes a hundred sets each year; the patterns never vary so she can knit them with her eyes closed, which she often does. It was odd now to see her concentrating on her knitting and nothing else.

"Oh," Tessa said in a strangely flat voice, "come in." She opened the door wider and without another word went back to her place on the stool. I stared at the policeman who came through the door and stood dripping on my doormat. Wrapped up in concern for Minnie, I'd forgotten that this was supposed to be Tessa's Greek god.

Not even his adoring mother would have called him gorgeous. His forehead came to a point over a too large nose. Small eyes lay hidden under heavy brows, like a young Neanderthal. He looked over the half wall into the living room and blinked at the women staring at him.

I frowned at Tessa. Had the snow blinded her or maybe a pom-pom had lodged in her eye? Nevertheless I was baffled by Tessa's rudeness, I jumped up blurting, "Uh, hello Constable. Is there anything wrong? Please come in. Can I take your coat?" I was stumbling over the words.

He blinked again mumbling, "No Ma'am. Um. Take a seat."

Surprised by his abrupt command, I obeyed. He took a step closer to the living room entry, reached inside his jacket and took out a small notebook. A pencil was tucked into the spiral binding. He pulled it out and licking the end said in a bored monotone, "I need all of your contact information. But first," he read from his notebook, "were you in the neighborhood between 3 and 7 today? And if so..."

I heard a faint gasp and guessed it was Minnie. His eyes shot up from the page looking around trying to see who'd been caught unaware by his question. Minnie was staring intensely at her lap her knitting forgotten. Everyone else looked like I felt, confused and mildly curious.

When he caught my eye, he blushed, looked at the ceiling; salvation, perhaps, then at the front door; or escape. He clutched his notebook and asked, "Did you? Have you? Uh, just answer the question!" he finished in a confused rush flipping to a new page.

Minnie plucked at her wool, Tessa continued to ignore him, knitting like a fury while I struggled to find something to say. I was relieved when George stood, taking charge, "May I see

...some ID, Constable whateveryournameis?" She asked with polite firmness. When George stands she commands attention. At just over 6 foot she met the Constable at eye level.

"Pardon?" he said, blushing crimson.

She raised her eyebrows and held out her hand, "Identification? Do you have any?"

"Oh yeah, sorry Bradley, I'm Constable Bradley." He repeated as he patted his pockets and, finding his warrant card, thrust it at George. He looked miserable as he squirmed under her gaze.

George eyed him as she studied the information carefully and after a long pause held it out to the group, "Anyone else care to examine it?"

There were murmurs and shakings of heads. This was George, the lawyer, in action. She was formidable. We were all as subdued as the poor Constable and more than happy she was taking the lead.

"Fine," she said handing back the card, "how may we be of assistance?"

Bradley looked like he would prefer to jump out of the nearest window. Finally, he muttered, "3 to 7, what were you doing, um, seeing?"

George paused for a moment, then asked, "You want to know what I was doing between 3 and 7 pm today?" Bradley nodded relieved. He didn't notice the mischief in her voice.

With a smirk she began, "My office is on Hastings Street about 4 blocks away. At 3 pm I was at work. I went for a coffee at 4:13 pm and was back at my desk at 4:37. My

DO THE KIDS HAVE MORE THAN 1 SITTER? IF NOT THIS SHOULD BE, SITTER'S (POSSESSIVE)

husband is out of town and my kids are at the sitters. I finished work early, drove to Pedro's, picked up my order of..."

Jen and I took our cue from George and said in unison, "Ceviche and a beef burrito." If she wasn't taking this police visit seriously, neither would we. A free evening for George always meant the same take out from her favorite Mexican restaurant.

We watched with amusement as poor Constable Bradley struggled to write down every unnecessary detail of George's Wednesday afternoon.

She continued in the same rapid fire delivery, "I drove home, parked, went to the kitchen, opened a Corona added the lime wedge from the ceviche, turned on the news, ate my dinner..."

Jen interjected, "Had an antacid."

"Yup!" George laughed, "Then left my house at 6:52 pm and arrived here at 6:56 pm."

Bradley was still writing when Jen winked at George conspiratorially and said, "No."

"No, what? Who said that?" he looked up.

"Me. I'm sorry. I'm just answering your question," Jen repeated sweetly, as though speaking to one of her children.

Bradley appeared to have forgotten his own question. I felt sorry for him, he seemed very young and totally out of his depth. I was trying to work out if George really remembered all the specific times she mentioned or if it was just to wind up the poor Constable. Knowing George and that she billed by the minute she probably could be that precise. Meanwhile I was having difficulty remembering what, if anything, I had done that day, it seemed a long time ago.

Bradley looked around the room. Tessa shook her head. With a sigh, he turned to Mariko. "No," she breathed in a voice as delicate as a leaf and bent her head, her cap of shining black hair hiding her face completely.

Minnie was picking at a fingernail. She too shook her head.

Poor Bradley looked pathetic. I took pity on him; he was only trying to do his job. I smiled brightly, "I work from home and have been here all day. In the afternoon I made scones for the group."

"Amy's scones, Yum!" Tessa cried, clapping her hands like a small child.

Bradley was momentarily distracted, looked at his notes and sighed, giving up, "Uh, I'll just need your contacts." One by one we gave him the information. When he got to me I asked, "Can you tell us what this is about?"

He stood a little straighter, suddenly pompous and self-important, "No ma'am. I'm not at liberty to say, ma'am." Stop calling me ma'am, I thought peevishly. Managing to sound only slightly put out, I asked, "Do you need anything else?"

He shook his head. I got up, "Then good night, Officer," I said and motioned to the front door. Closing it behind him I headed to the kitchen for the scones and a big pot of tea.

It was quiet when I returned to the living room with the tray.

"What do you think that was about?" Jen finally asked.

"I have no idea," George replied, "but I don't think that's the last we'll see of the police."

I agreed, "It's hard to believe that anyone can be that inept. I wonder what criminals make of him."

"Well, he didn't give anything away," Jen added kindly.

"That's true," George said picking up her knitting and smiling, "but the real question is one that only Tessa can answer. I get that your concept of gorgeous may be different from mine but I think we can all agree that Constable Bradley is by no one's definition, handsome."

"Obviously not him," Tessa replied, continuing to knit. "There was another man, maybe we just got the Bad Cop, not the Good Cop, you know like in TV shows," she sighed.

George ignored her, reassuring the group, "I don't suppose that whatever happened can be too bad if they are sending out the infant police force. I mean he didn't even find out if any of us really saw or heard anything. All I told him was what I was doing." She paused grinning, "Do you ~~supposed~~ he got it all down in his notebook?" *SUPPOSE*

I tried to recall the details of my day as I handed round the tea and conversation became general and relaxed. Even Minnie looked better after a few sips. I smiled, loving the fact that these women, now my close friends were brought into my life by knitting. There's no question that we would never have met without that link. I looked at them with affection. Normally our knit nights were full of laughter and fun. Tonight was different, first, there was Minnie's strange behavior and now a visit from the police.

CHAPTER 2

Minnie is the oldest member of the group and with me, a founder. She is a self-appointed neighborhood welcoming committee and mother figure. Without her, the group would not exist. Shortly after I moved into the area she came by late one afternoon with a fresh batch of cookies and introduced herself. I was sitting on my front porch knitting while watching a bunch of 6-year-olds play bumble bee soccer in the schoolyard across the street. We talked and found we had a lot in common despite our age difference. She was delighted to find another knitter and we began meeting up on soccer nights, laughing at the kids who followed the ball like bees to honey, knitting and becoming good friends. She's ageless and adorable, with her bottle blonde bouffant to the t-shirts she wears festooned with sparkles and clinging just a bit too tightly Minnie is well past her best before date but she doesn't care and enjoys life immensely.

Neither of us knew Tessa until she ran by one day. It was half time on the soccer pitch and Minnie was holding up her knitting, an afghan she was examining for the hole she knew was lurking somewhere. I got out of my chair to help in the search when I noticed Tessa. She was jogging in place on the sidewalk in front of my house, staring. When she caught my eye she waved, called out a breathless hello and loped up my steps, sweaty and gasping.

"Oooh knitters, my favorite people!" she exclaimed and within minutes established who we were, that we regularly met to knit and invited herself to join us. Soon other knitters started appearing till there were eight of us. It still amazes me that all these women live within a few blocks and yet we never knew that we shared a common craft.

Jen and George were already good friends and came as one connecting with Tessa through their shared cleaning lady.

Tessa brought Meg who introduced us to Claire. And finally, there was Mariko, Minnie's exchange student. Mariko is very prim and proper with starched collars and a soft musical voice. Like a porcelain figurine, she looks fragile and yet designs and makes outlandish clothing and knitwear for dolls. Her creations are bizarre, in the style of Harajuku outfits from the streets of Tokyo and complex Manga costumes. As fast as she can make them she sends them back to Japan for sale. Minnie says that Mariko makes quite a lot of money from them.

Meg met Tessa at the casino where they both occasionally work. Tessa moonlights from time to time as a croupier but I've never been able to understand exactly what Meg does, except that it involves card counting scams. Meg's away for a year on sabbatical from her job as a professor of advanced mathematics. While she plans to return in the summer I have my doubts. She is working on a postdoctoral paper on mathematics in music that will become a book if the funding holds out. The fact that she is attached to the Sorbonne in Paris and loving every minute makes me think she will find the funding, the book will take longer than planned, and that leaving Paris in summer is not in the cards. We all envy her and miss her expertise. She is the one we turn to when we have a question, a gifted teacher who can easily explain the most intricate pattern.

Soon after Meg joined she asked if she could bring Claire, her travel guru. Claire is a globe-trotting go-getter, full of energy. She is sleek and glossy and knits an endless supply of scarves. As a tour organizer for an ecological travel company, her specialty is high-end travel for small groups. Currently, she is in Wales scouting a three-week circumnavigation of Anglesey by foot, cycle, and kayak for a group of techies. From time to time she sends emails. The latest, "I'm coasteering!" showed a picture of her in helmet, harness, and bikini scaling a small cliff from the sea. I envy her, Tessa wants to go with her, Minnie just shakes her head in wistful

14

amazement, Jen and Mariko nod and smile while George is adamant, "She's crazy!"

George and Claire are total opposites though that doesn't hinder their friendship. When Claire leaves town for a weekend her luggage is a shoulder bag packed with a pair of underwear and a toothbrush. George has lists; very detailed alphabetical lists. When George got a smart phone the first thing she did, even before her first call, was to input her lists to Notes. Since then she has become addicted to a post-it notes app. I think she may be a bit too organized. Before a camping trip last summer she called, did I know where she could get a pink sleeping bag. As it happened I had one in my basement that I said she could borrow. When I took it over the next day I saw four piles of camping gear, blue for her husband Tim, pink for her and orange and green for each of her two boys. George explained that each of them was assigned a color. "This way we won't use someone else's towel or spoon by mistake," she explained.

When I told her best friend, Jen, the story she laughed, "In my family, I'm lucky if I remember to pack one towel for the four of us!"

"What happens when your two families go camping together?"

Jen giggled, "its perfect, George brings a purple pile of extras for us."

Best friends, George and Jen met when they were both pregnant with their first child. During prenatal classes, they bonded. When they became pregnant for the second time, they gave birth within days of each other. George has 2 boys, Jen 2 girls. While the kids may one day be great friends at 8 and 6 it is more like WWIII whenever they have a play date.

Unlike George, Jen keeps track of her busy life with old-fashioned paper sticky notes. Her refrigerator looks like a scaly reptile with messages stuck at random over the entire surface. There seems to be no order in their placement and though George has tried to get her to go electronic, Jen happily carries on sticking and re-sticking errant notes. She is one of the kindest people I know and knows everyone in the town. Before becoming a stay at home mom and full-time volunteer for everything from her kid's school to the local 'clean the stream' team, she worked as the go-to person on the local paper writing features, taking photos of prize winners and signing up advertisers. Now that her girls are both in school she hints she may go back to the paper part time. I hope she does as the news and local coverage were better when she was on board.

Tessa also hopes she goes back as Jen always gave Tessa the best rates and full coverage when she held her annual trunk shows. The current guy is more interested in football than fashion Tessa says with disgust.

Tessa is an exotic bird in our little corner of Port Oxford. Not only does she look exotic with gorgeous olive skin, almond shaped eyes and a wide mouth usually a brilliant scarlet she cultivates an air of mystery. First, there is her full name, Contessa Monita O'Grady, a delicious mix of Italian, Spanish, and Irish. It's her real name, I've seen her passport.

For fun she works as a croupier occasionally, that's where she met Meg. The casino loves it when she agrees to take the midnight shift, her table is always full.
"It's fun! You meet such bizarre people and the tips are ridiculous," she confided recently. As in every other part of her life, she is over-the-top. I've seen her pass through a crowded room like a queen and later sit on the front steps of the courthouse to share a sandwich with a homeless guy. She and I quickly became friends with much in common, both single, in our early thirties and self-employed at jobs we love.

Knitting is her passion and profession. Her business card reads Contessa O'Grady, Bespoke Knitwear. When I read it I had no idea what 'bespoke' meant. She explained, "I once knew an English guy who was a bespoke shirtmaker. It is the term for custom made, a one of a kind garment. That's exactly what I do and yet half my clients don't know what it means." I wondered about the shirtmaker and how long he lasted in her very long string of admirers. While men are captivated by her, I have to admit her attention span is short.

She is the Picasso of knitting, an eccentric genius. She's also one hell of a businesswoman. Working only on commission, she demands complete autonomy and refuses any job she feels unworthy of her talents.

Currently, she is working on a wrap for one of the Real Housewives of Vancouver. Tessa says the woman is a complete waste of space but that when she saw the evening gown for which a matching shawl was commissioned, she agreed. She told me she couldn't help herself, "The dress is fantastic. It looks like Monet's water lilies, I want to swim in the fabric, so I agreed but I'm charging her double just because she's such a drip." Tonight was the first time I'd seen of the project and I was having trouble visualizing how the mauve and brown tweed wool was going to work with a dress featuring yards of sea-green chiffon and tulle.

I watched Tessa deep in her work, surrounded by a mound of seaweed colored fluff. Jen and George were talking about schooling while Minnie and Mariko were quietly knitting. Minnie looked more relaxed I was relieved to see.

Suddenly Tessa looked up, her head tilted like an alert bird, "Listen," she said.
Again there was the crunch of footsteps on my stairs followed by a firm knock. At this time of night I guessed it could only

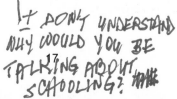

I DON'T UNDERSTAND WHY WOULD YOU BE TALKING ABOUT SCHOOLING?

17

be the police again, I looked at Minnie. She was composed and even gave me a slight smile.

Tessa stared at me, "You get it," she murmured, "I had my chance."

I looked at her suspiciously and went to open the door.

"Oh," I breathed.

He looked away, listening to a question from someone further down the block. I blushed like a teenager then held my breath and waited for him to turn around staring at a tiny curl that fell over his ear.

He called down to an officer, something about continuing to the next street. There was a further query. He turned to face me, "Sorry. I'll be back," he said quickly and bounded down the stairs. Even though he was clearly exasperated, his voice was a deep baritone, it rang a bell I felt in my toes.

CHAPTER 3

I closed the door, leaning my back against it and exhaled, "Oh my." I said louder than I intended. When I entered the room, everyone was staring at me except Tessa who didn't even look up, saying, "Didn't I tell you?"
I sat, sending the chair rocking madly.

"He said, 'I'll be back,' just like the Terminator," Jen sparkled, "this is good!"

I tried to explain, "Sorry, wait till you see him," I said breathlessly, "this guy is ..." I couldn't finish the sentence. Pulling myself together I tried again, "He's like movie star gorgeous. I mean what would you do if you opened the door and standing there was Brad Pitt or the guy that plays the wolfman..." I trailed off helplessly.

Tessa looked at me, one eyebrow arched, "Me? I'd change."

Change? Morph into Aphrodite? "What are you talking about?"

WHY ARE THERE ALWAYS SO MANY SPACES?

Then I followed her eyes and looked down. Yikes! This was knit night, a bunch of women sitting around chatting. I was dressed for comfort in a pair of yoga pants, thick wooly socks, and my favorite knit night t-shirt. While I loved the shirt I was aware that it was in no way fashionable or flattering. Black with huge orange lettering it reads Swatches are for Sissies. I wear it on knit nights proudly and sheepishly.
I love it because it was a gift from the group at Christmas, the result of one specific project, a top down sweater that I was unraveling for the third time. When Tessa, the master of improvised knitting seriously suggested that I should try knitting a test swatch, I laughed. "Swatches are boring," I

explained, "knitting little measured squares reminds me of granny afghans."

"So you'd rather re-knit something four times than figure out the sizing first?" she asked. She was right of course, it was irrational.

In a daze, I looked at the scones. My subconscious knew exactly what it intended as I picked one up, slathered it with strawberry jam and bit into it. Jam gushed down my shirt. "Oops," I said not very convincingly, my complexion matching the jam. Tessa narrowed her eyes and grinned.

"Now you'll have to change," Jen announced.

"Was there ever any question?" George asked laughing.

I stood up and stumbled in my rush into the hall, Tessa following.
"I'll help," she said and slipped through my bedroom door before I could close it.

"Tessa, I don't need any help. I only need to change into a clean shirt."
Tessa stood with her hands on her hips. "Are you interested or not?"

"Not! He's way out of my league!"

"Bollocks! We need to hurry, he could be back at any time."

I conceded, "I guess it wouldn't hurt to try to look nice."

I sat on the bed as she started flipping through the hangers of clothes in my closet muttering, "Too blah, might work, good grief!"

Then it struck me. What if he noticed I changed? What would he think? Was it too late to brazen it out and wear the damn t-shirt? I watched glumly, as the jam soaked through, sticking to my skin. Too late now, I pulled the shirt off and threw it into the corner.

"Stand up. Let's take a look at you." She turned me around, away from the mirror; her hands were on my shoulders giving me a little squeeze, "Relax. Trust me."

I knew what I looked like. Tall with a long waist that made my legs look short and a little too much padding around the hips. Shoulder length hair alternating between edgy, when newly cut and boring when too long. Right now it was too long and I'd scraped it back into an elastic. Green eyes with a hint of laugh lines at the edges, not horrible but not outstanding either.

"Ok, the yoga pants are good, they fit, not too tight and they don't sag so they'll work." She pointed, "There's jam on your bra." She handed me a white cotton sports bra, "Put this on."

"I can't go out in that!" I wailed.

"Of course not," she said calmly.

Mutely, I changed into the bra. In no way was this sexy. The cut was high on my chest and my breasts were flattened. I stood in the centre of the room, black pants, white bra top, "This is ridiculous. So what if he is gorgeous. I don't know what I'm thinking. Give me my t shirt. I'm not dressing special for someone I've never met."

"You can't wear the t-shirt. Period. Anyway, you aren't dressing for him, this is for you." Tessa was rummaging in the back of my closet. I could hear her grumbling over the rattle of hangers.

"For me?"   *looked fabulous*

She ignored me/ "Perfect! I knew you would have kept this,"
she cried as she pulled out a sarong.   It was a long length of
batik cotton that I'd bought in Bali, one of those things that at
the time look fabulous.   I'd worn it every day to the beach
delighted at the way the orange, brown and purple swirls
covered and flattered my bathing suit clad body. When I got
home I realized that what was beautiful in Bali was garish in
Port Oxford.   It lived in the back of my closet, a forgotten
travel trophy.

Tessa turned me, "Raise your arms."   I did so with a silent
appeal to heaven, Tessa can wear this kind of stuff, I can't.

"Ok, where's your makeup?" she asked after she finished
wrapping and tucking the long length of fabric around me.

"No, no makeup. I'll look like I'm trying"

"Aren't you? Where did you get this purple," she demanded,
waving the liner in my face.

"I don't know, I never wear it."

"I realize that," she muttered as she applied it to my eyes, "it's
perfect. Now look in the mirror."

I gazed at a vision that vaguely resembled me, a fabulous
me. Somehow she had twisted and draped the sarong into a
blouse. It covered my arms to my elbows, had a cowl neck
and draped over my hips covering any lumps along the way.
Because it was folded and tucked the colors weren't garish at
all.   Instead, they swirled into a sunset. It was in no way
provocative, no cleavage, not clingy yet it made me feel
beautiful and sexy.

"Can I lift my arms or will it fall apart?"

"You can do anything but tango" she replied serenely.

I looked closely at my face. Something was different, in a good way. The barest hint of blush made my cheeks look like they actually had bones and a thin streak of purple at my lower lash line gave my eyes a unique shape, wide and large. Suddenly it came to me that this, caring about how I looked, was something I hadn't done in a long time.

Tessa must have guessed I was a little embarrassed, "It's ok, remember you're not dressing for him, men don't notice clothes anyway. You're dressing for yourself. Think of it this way. Clothes are supposed to make you happy and give you confidence. When that doesn't happen you need a wardrobe overhaul, not for him or me or anyone but yourself."

I nodded.

"Your closet is a disaster but we'll talk about that later. Right now you need to get back to the living room."

I nodded again; I felt like a bobble head doll.

Every eye was on me as I came out the door. "Va Va Va Voom!" Jen cried to George's wolf whistle. Suddenly all the tension in me floated away, these were my friends and I felt like a movie star. I laughed and hammed it up, mincing my steps and posing for imaginary photographers. I threw a kiss to Tessa as she took a mock bow.

Mariko reached out to touch the sarong's fabric and even Minnie smiled.
I sat and looked down to ensure that no stray bits of fabric came loose. I couldn't concentrate and knew if I started to knit I'd be ripping it all out later so I drank my tea.

By the time he returned, I was as ready as I'd ever be. Nervousness makes me clumsy so I took care getting up to answer the door.

"Hello, I was here earlier and didn't introduce myself," he said, "Inspector Sommerville."

When I didn't say anything he continued, "And you are?" "Amy," it came out as a whisper so I cleared my throat, "Amy. Amy Stevens." That was better.

"Great. I believe you spoke with my Constable earlier?"

I heard a sniff and a snicker. So did Sommerville. He looked around, so did I. The group was a picture of innocence.

He looked at his notes, "Yes, well, I understand that all of you got here around 7. I need to confirm that and whether you may have heard or seen anything out of the ordinary between 3 and 7."

George spoke first, "Really Inspector! This is ridiculous."

He didn't blush or stammer, like his constable. He waited.

"Unless you tell us what is going on I don't think we can't tell you anything more than we told Bradface," she said.

Jen was more apologetic, she said smoothly, "Your Constable, Bradley, I think his name was, didn't tell us anything but I know we would all like to help."

"I see," he took a deep breath, and ran his fingers down his jaw, "there has been an incident at 4147 Eaton. We need to know, as quickly as possible," he said with emphasis, "what time you arrived here and if you saw anyone or a car or heard anything around that house between 3 and 7."

This sounded serious.   "I can answer the first question, everyone arrived at almost the same time, within 10 minutes of 7."

"Everyone confirm that?" he asked the group. They nodded as the Inspector made a note.

I thought for a moment, I was 4116 Hudson,   Eaton ran parallel on the other side of the playground.   "Minnie, you're on Eaton, what number are you?"

Minnie looked flustered and muttered, "4107."

Sommerville turned to her, checking his notepad, "You are Ms. Grant?" he asked.

"Yes," she whispered.

He jotted a note in his book. He looked at her appraisingly, then continued writing. "And I understand from the notes that you were home before you came here and you didn't see or hear anything?"
It wasn't an accusation but there was an uncomfortable pause while Minnie clasped and unclasped her hands. Finally, she shook her head.

George broke the silence, "Between 3 and 7 you said?"

Sommerville turned to her and nodded.

 "I was at work and then home but I saw nothing out of the ordinary."

As he scanned each of the others, they said the same.   No one had noticed anything.

He turned his attention to me, "And you, Ms. Stevens?"

"Well, I'm not sure." I stared at my hands trying to think. Ever since Constable Bradley had asked the same question a faint bell had gone off in my brain, "I've been home all day and I can't think of anything offhand, but..." I hesitated. There was something, something small, probably insignificant. I couldn't quite put my finger on it. The Inspector waited patiently and I finally shrugged, "I'm sure it's nothing." I felt like an idiot, he must think I was trying to make myself important.

Tessa stood abruptly, "If you are through with the rest of us, its time to go. We'll just get our things and get out of your way."
Sommerville shrugged, "I've got your contact info so we're good for now. We'll be in touch later if we need any formal statements."

Tessa passed out coats adding, "I'm sure Amy will remember what is bothering her if you stay and give her a little more time."

I blushed, could she be any less subtle? I tried to get up but it really was very crowded. So I sat back and tried to think. Whatever it was I was trying to remember, deep down I also knew it must be insignificant.

Tessa shepherded everyone out the door cutting off prolonged farewells. "Sommerville," she called as she left, "help yourself to a scone, Amy made them and I think the tea is still hot."

He smiled as he watched the pom-poms on her hat bounce down the stairs. "Is she always like that?"

"Oh yes," I didn't even need to ask what he meant. When he grinned in response I was glad I was already sitting down. He hung his coat on a newly vacant hook and came into the room.

He SAID

"Do you mind?" pointing at the tray. He sat opposite me, poured some tea and took a scone adding lots of jam and cream. I smiled as he ate it with relish.

"Have another," I offered? I was quite enjoying watching him eat.

THESE SPACES !!

"I will, thanks." He relaxed into the chair while he ate and looked around the room. He wasn't a large man, probably just around 6'. Not noticeably muscular, he was well built, solid. I put his age in his early 40's. He had a full head of dark brown hair with a touch of gray at the temples. It was tied with a leather thong in a rough ponytail, stray tendrils curled over his collar and around his ears. His clothes fit well and had obviously been bought for comfort, not style. Then I saw his shoes. They were beautiful. Somehow I knew they were handmade. I smiled.

AS IN UNDERWEAR ??

"Do you remember?" he asked, watching me.

"What?" I tried to concentrate by staring at the hand stitching on his shoes.

"Sorry, do you remember what you mentioned earlier?" he reminded me.

"No, I'm the one who should be sorry. I just can't seem to put my finger on it. The more I think about it the more I think it was nothing special, probably nothing at all."

He got up, "I really have to go, lots more people to see. I don't want to push you. Why don't you think about it and I'll give you my card," he said as he dug out his wallet, "you can call me when it comes back to you."
I stood up as well, the batik fabric floating gracefully around me. He handed me his card and I took it with two hands. He pulled on his coat, "Thanks for the scones and tea, it's going to be long night."

On the porch, he pointed to the house opposite, across the schoolyard and down three. "4147, that's the house. Do you know the people that live there?"

"Sorry, I don't think so."

"Well, If you think of anything, no matter how small, call. Thanks again.   Scones are much better than donuts," he grinned.

I watched until he disappeared down the street then looked over at the house. Even though there was nothing except the fenced school grounds between us, the house seemed very far away and I'd never really paid any attention to it. Tonight it was lit up like a Christmas tree.   I closed the door remembering the sound of his voice. It seemed to echo in the hall.   Then I turn over his card and read, Inspector Jackson Sommerville, Homicide.

TURNED

CHAPTER 4

[handwritten: THOUGHT IT WAS ON MINNIE'S BLOCK (pg 25)]

[handwritten: why is this word here?]

Homicide! I leaned against the front door. Here. On my block. I'd thought it was something mundane like burglary or car theft. But murder! And practically on my doorstep. I could see the victim's house from my porch. I shivered.

Locking the deadbolt instantly made me feel safer as I leaned against the solid wood door and began to think. Should I be worried? Nervously I checked the lock was secure. Was a madman loose in the neighborhood? No, the police would have said something, someone, the Inspector would have given a warning. He already knew that all my friends lived nearby, he had their addresses. Surely, they wouldn't have been allowed to walk home if there was a threat in the area. Since that made sense, I was relieved. I felt better as I speculated, it must be an inside job. The police must already believe that the murderer and victim knew each other. It could even be an accident or domestic dispute for all I knew. They were simply going door-to-door asking to find any witnesses. Since I had nothing in common with the victim but our address, I felt safe. I relaxed as I worked out these simple details.

Curiosity got to me. There were a thousand questions I should have asked and I hadn't asked one, nothing, nada. What an idiot! Bewitched by his looks, I had practically drooled at the man. Was there such a thing as a police groupie? Should I start a club? The Jack Pack? Smiling, I gave myself a mental shake. He was cute, okay gorgeous, and I was a grown woman who had better start acting like one. Time to regroup. With a rueful grin I put aside the biggest most burning question of all, was he married? Instead I focussed on the homicide.

What should I have asked? The first was pretty basic, was it murder or an accident? Any other questions I had, like all of them; who, what, when, how, and why would have to wait till the news hit the paper. It was Wednesday, the next edition of our local paper wasn't until Saturday. It might be a big enough incident to be in the Metro Vancouver papers, it really depended on the luridness. But it would definitely be covered by our little town paper. For the Port Oxford News or PON as it was known this was very big news. Nothing ever happened in Port Oxford, nothing like this anyway. I needed more facts, more information but I'd have to wait till Saturday. Meanwhile, I would try to remember my 'memory.' I was sure it was something to do with my house. Even to me sounded weird. What could something in my house have to do with a murder a block away? *EARLIER YOU SAID IT WAS ON YOUR BLOCK*

I looked down the hall seeing the entire house from where I stood. Tonight it felt the same as always, welcoming, secure.

Then I shivered, I was cold. A freezing draft was sneaking up my spine from around the door, reminding me that I had meant to change the weatherstripping in the fall. I giggled nervously, weather stripping wouldn't keep out a murderer. Giving myself a shake I checked again that the door was bolted before clearing away the debris from knit night.

I walked down the hall with the dishes balanced carefully in my hands feeling the warmth of the house embrace me. This was a home of good memories, family memories. My grandparents built it in 1953 and lived in it until the early 70's when my father met and married my mother and moved a few miles away. Within a year my grandparents retired to a little bungalow in Sechelt leaving the house to be rented out. Five years ago when my grandfather passed away my father offered it to me at a bargain price. It's small and sturdy and I love it, not only because of the link with my beloved grandfather. It was also a shrewd investment, as land prices have skyrocketed in this small community on the outskirts of Vancouver.

& as you on Hudson
Minnie on Eaton

PG 29 says murder on your block.
Pg 30 says it's a block away 30

My house sits on a large lot with a flight of stairs leading from the sidewalk to a covered front porch that runs the entire width, 24 feet. I know the exact measurement because each main room, except the kitchen, is a perfect 10x 10-foot cube. The front door opens into a 4' wide hall, running straight to the back porch. On the left is the living room, with 9' ceilings like the whole house. The entrance into the room is wide and on either side, a wall comes up halfway to form a shelf. A perfect landing zone for keys, groceries and plants. Decorating such a small living room is challenging. A low bookcase on the far wall sits under a wall mounted TV. The flat screen is covered with a painting of mine on a sliding panel, a forest scene in fall colors. All the furniture is a mixture of patterns and colors, mostly in creams and dark earthy reds and browns. No two pieces are the same and somehow it is undemanding without being boring. I'm an artist, color is important to me.

Down the hall I passed every room, loving the colors and style. Everything in the home was mine, my choice, design and mostly my execution. I had stripped wallpaper, filled holes and painted till I got it right.

Opposite the living room is my bedroom. Since the room also faces the street, noise can be a problem. When I moved in I replaced all the windows. The old wood sash ones were painted shut or so stuck that it was hazardous to try to open them. The new windows help with soundproofing and keep the rooms warm in winter.

I designed the bedroom as a flower garden. One wall is a deep eggplant and the rest pale green. The bed has a white frame and the comforter a riot of wildflowers in full colors. A small white nightstand and dresser are the only other furniture. Farther down the hall is the bath with the original claw foot tub. The walls are painted and papered in a bold bamboo pattern. The hall empties into the kitchen with my studio on the left. The kitchen is the largest room only because the 10x10 is expanded by the width of the hall. It is the heart of the house with the original cupboards, farmhouse sink and a walk-in pantry all painted in shades of apricot to pumpkin. I checked the back door lock, turned off the light and went to bed.

The sun was streaming through my kitchen window the next morning. The play of colors through a stained glass piano window saved during my renovations banished the fatigue I felt after a dream filled and restless night. All I could remember was watching a soccer game in which both teams wore black hoodies. It was frightening and yet I could not turn away.

I made myself a cup of coffee and moved a chair into the sunlight feeling it warm me deep inside. I gave up trying to figure out what my dream meant. That's what dreams are, just plain weird. I stood, pushed the chair back into place and went to the fridge for some yogurt and fruit for breakfast.

It was still early when Tessa called, "Is he still there?" she asked.

I could hear the grin in her voice; subtlety is not a strong point with Tessa. I didn't have to ask who she was talking about.

"No, is he there?" I asked.

"Ha!" she laughed. "I told you I had my chance and that was Blobface!"

"His name is Bradley and he can't help what he looks like."

"Whatever. Tell me all about the crime and Mr. Dish."
"Actually I don't know anything," I admitted, telling her about my mental block of the night before.

"And you're suggesting you aren't interested. Huh, " she teased. "So what did happen?"

"Not much. He ate the scones and that was it. By the way, I had the devil of a time unwrapping myself from that sarong." I smiled.

"Well, I assumed you'd have help," she said mischievously.

I can never win with Tessa and laughed, "So are you coming over?"

"Any scones left?"

"No, he likes scones better than donuts."

"Ah! He has good taste! Oh well, I did better than you in the information department. Don't you want to hear what I found out?"

"I'm all ears."

"The 'incident' is actually a suspicious death!" she said dramatically.

"I know. The Inspector is with Homicide."

"Aren't you on a first name basis yet?"

Only in my mind. "Just get on with it! "

"The dead guy is Frank Slinger. Ever heard of him?"

"No, I don't think so. How do you know his name?"

"I asked another constable on my way home."

Why couldn't I have been on the ball? Making up for lost time I asked, "What did he look like? I don't know the name but I may have noticed him around."

"I used to see him on my runs. He was always walking in the neighborhood so you might remember him, he is, or was, medium height, with kind of a big head. Not much hair and big square glasses."

"That sort of rings a bell. Did he carry a big scruffy bag?" I was picturing the bag more than the man.
"Yes, that's the one. The bag is an old letter carrier bag. I figure he is a retired postal worker."

"How do you work that out, Sherlock? I mean he could have picked the bag up at a garage sale or something."

Tessa explained patiently, "Well, I don't know this for a fact but those bags are government property and you don't just pick one up at a junk store so I think he was a postie and just forgot, so to speak, to turn it in when he retired."

"I guess so but why do you think he's retired?"

"Because whenever I've seen him, the bag was full groceries."

"Sounds like you are jumping to conclusions, Miss Marple. But I'll grant you that it's a good deduction. What else have you guessed?"

"He seems to be one of the good guys. He volunteers as a driver for the cancer clinic and has an overweight cat. Oh, and he's a car buff."

I was astonished. "Tessa, really, how did you get all this? It's not even 10 am! "

"Once I knew which house it was, it was easy," she said smugly.

"You're going have to spell it out for me, I'm a little tired this morning," I begged.

"He drives that old brown sedan, I think it's a Corolla. It's always parked out front. Don't tell me you haven't seen it. It's the one with the Cancer Foundation Driver decal on the door!"

"No," I said honestly, "I guess I just don't notice those kinds of things."

She was exasperated, "What do you do all day?"

I didn't say that I don't spend my time snooping on the neighbours. "I think I know about the cat." I knew of one in neighborhood that was seriously overweight. I didn't add that I was probably the source of his weight problem, me and the tidbits I left out. "What about the car, a car buff who drives a Corolla? No way!"

"Yes, way! On my run today I just happened to go down his lane and his garage was open. The floor is painted in a black and white checkered racing pattern. He must be a car nut. And," she added significantly, "there is a huge car and a workshop with tools and oil cans and car stuff."

"You just happened to run down his lane, today? Really?" Tessa didn't reply so I gave in, "Ok, what kind of car is it?" I asked, even though I knew what her answer would be.

"I couldn't get close, that whole side of the lane was taped off. All I could see was that it is big and black." Tessa only cares if a car starts on the first try, and goes forward and backward, model names mean nothing.

"Come over for coffee."

"I can't. I have to meet with the witch of Vancouver. She says she has a new idea for her wrap. I can't wait to tell her no. "

"I bet no one has ever said no to her."

"Yeah, I'm hoping for a full-on tantrum. Want to come and watch?" She giggled.

"No," I hesitated, actually I would have liked to, "I've never met a reality show person but I'll have to pass I've got things to do here. Maybe I'll even go for a walk."

"You should do that. And while you are checking out Slinger's place, drop in on Minnie, she was a little strange last night."

I ignored her comment about the reason for a walk. "You noticed too. I don't think Minnie knit a single row and usually, she finishes a whole scarf at knit night." I paused, "You don't think she is sick, do you?"

"She looked fine by the end of the evening and Mariko made sure she got home safe but it won't hurt to drop over and see. You could borrow a cup of something"

I laughed, "Like what?"

"You'll think of something," she said and rang off.

CHAPTER 5

That was interesting; Tessa was concerned about Minnie too. It wasn't just my imagination. I planned to check in on her. I could borrow a cup of courage from Minnie in case I met up with the Inspector when I wandered down her lane to Slinger's house.

PREVIOUSLY YOU SPELLED IT W/ A U

Ours is an old neighborhood. Many of the homes were built about the same time as mine with wood siding and deep front porches. There are also ones built in the 70's, the ones we call Vancouver Specials. They resemble 2 story shoe boxes and are covered in stucco. Minnie lives in one of the latter. Down the street from her, Slinger's seemed to be similar to mine, only larger. Their street, Eaton and mine, Hudson run parallel. Between them, blocking my view of Minnie's house, is the grammar school, a red brick three-story structure that was built in the '40's and is graceful and ageless, at least from the outside. Ivy covers the side facing me with the classroom windows cut out of the thick carpet of leaves. At the front, the huge stone stairway is a natural gathering place for mothers and their kids while at the back there is a playground on the tarmac. Beyond that are the gravel and grass playing fields lined with high fencing. I look onto those fields through the link fencing. When I first moved in I was concerned that a school full of boisterous elementary kids would interrupt my work. But within a short time I found their noise and the schedule of bells a soothing way to structure my day.

I finished my breakfast and dressed, noting that it would be recess soon. I put on my best jeans, half boots and a car coat with a hood in forest green. I told myself I wasn't planning on running into anyone but it never hurts to look nice. And if I did accidentally meet Inspector Sommerville I remembered Tessa's advice. This was for me, I needed all the confidence I could muster, if nothing else, to keep from drooling. Standing on my front porch I looked across the field to Slinger's house. There was only one car in front. It didn't look like a police car and it wasn't brown so it wasn't Slingers. The barricades and tape I'd seen last night were gone. Maybe they had all the information they needed from the house. Even so, it seemed awfully quiet. In movies, there is always miles of crime scene tape with officers and forensic people swarming over the place for days. Today seemed like a typically quiet day in the neighborhood.

I headed down the stairs. My house is about mid-block and although it is slightly shorter to go around the front of the school to Minnie's, I took the longer route.

The sleet of last night had turned to a light misty rain and gray clouds filled the sky. I pulled up my hood slowing as I passed in front of Slinger's house. It was eerie. There was no one about the place. Probably the awful weather was keeping people indoors. Even so, I expected a few nosey parkers, not that I considered myself one, I grinned. There was a sign posted on the front door that I couldn't read from the street. No curtains twitched, the house looked deserted. Should I go up the steps to check it out? Before I changed my mind I ran, as quietly as I could, up the stairs and read, 'Crime Scene, Do Not Enter. All police personnel should be aware of the proximity to the schoolyard and use the rear door for access.'

How thoughtful. Was this Jack's idea? I ran back to the street and walked quickly to Minnie's.

Mariko was at school, I knew. She was attending an English as a Second Language school though in her case it seemed an excruciatingly slow process. That didn't bother Minnie, she and Mariko got along very well. Minnie did all the talking and Mariko did all the listening, it suited them both. I walked up her steps and rang the bell. There was no reply. I rang again. Since Minnie is nearly always home in the daytime, I was surprised.

I decided to check and see if her car was out back. Her garage was empty and that relieved me somewhat. She must be ok if she was out shopping. Trying to look casual, I wandered down the lane toward Slinger's house. The barrier that Tessa described was gone. In its place, yellow tape was strung across the open garage door and there was a car covered with a thick cotton tarp. As I neared, I gasped. Even with the tarp on I knew that shape. A 1957 Bel Air Chevrolet.

"A 57 and black too," I breathed and took an involuntary step towards it.

"How do you know that?" a voice asked from behind me. It was Inspector Jackson Sommerville. Cripes! Of all the luck, I took a deep breath and stood a little straighter, without turning I said, "so it is a '57."

His voice was a little rougher, more insistent, "You can't see the car," he was right, the car was completely covered by the tarp, "and yet you know the year and color and I'm sure you'll be able to tell me the make and model too."

Subdued, I nodded, so.

"You must have known Slinger," he said staring at me intently, "we know that he kept this car under lock and key and in fact rarely took it out of the garage. So I'll ask again, how do you know this car?"

Shaken, I replied, "I don't, not really. Let me explain."

He held up his hand, "Wait," he said and reached into his pocket pulling out a phone, "now, speak clearly."

I felt so guilty. I hadn't done anything, didn't know anything and yet staring at that little black screen with the red microphone blinking I found it hard to think straight.

I took a deep breath, "I don't know this particular car, I've never seen it. But, I do know a 57 Chevrolet Bel Air Coupe. How could anyone mistake those tail-fins? Even under the tarp. My father had a passion for them. He restored one and drove it till the day he died. I grew up with it."

"And the fact that it is black?"

I'd have to tell him about Tessa. She can fend for herself I decided, I was in enough trouble. "Tessa, my friend, from knitting, she mentioned that she saw an old black car out back." He looked skeptical. I didn't blame him. I didn't make sense to me either. "Tessa doesn't know anything about cars," I added helpfully, if incoherently.

He paused then switched off the phone.

I pointed to the tarp, "Can I?" and motioned to peel it back.

"No. I will," he said and picked up a corner so that I could peek.

I forgot about Sommerville, staring at the car, a million memories of my Dad flooding me. I could see him, a can of wax in his hand lovingly rubbing the surface of the car.

"It's a beauty," I said. "Slinger must have loved this car. The only polish job I've seen that was better was my Dad's. He spent hours at it, hours that we talked, long involved conversations ranging from corn flakes to the cosmos." I stopped, the Inspector was a good listener. "Anyway, my dad's was blue, Marlin Blue. I like it better than this, black makes it look like a hearse." I blushed, "Sorry that was tactless," I mumbled.

"Not to me," he replied. I looked at him. As a cop that was probably true but I hoped he wasn't insensitive, no longer caring about the people he investigated.

He was staring at the car. I looked away quickly when he turned back to me asking, "How did you come to be walking this way?"

It seemed pointless not to tell the truth, "I wanted to have a look at the house."

"Why?'

"Nothing special, just curiosity."

He looked at me intently, I could feel his eyes boring into me. This must be how real criminals feel under interrogation.

"Have you remembered what you heard or saw?" he asked. He was relentless.

"Uh, no," I shook my head and turned to stare at the car, at least then my tongue seemed to be able to obey my thoughts, "no flashes of brilliance in the night. Please don't expect anything, really." Now I was embarrassed, I honestly couldn't remember what it was. The more I tried to tie down the memory the more insignificant I felt it was. He probably thought I was making something up for his benefit. Or he hoped it was some vital fact that would miraculously solve the case. Either way he was doomed to be disappointed, I was sure. I wanted to crawl away and hide. Where was a big black hole when you needed one?

"Are you're sure you didn't know Frank Slinger?"

"No, why do you think I should?"

He looked at me closely, but did not to elaborate, "Don't let me interrupt your walk." He took a garage opener out of his pocket and clicked the door shut then turned back to the house.

I felt flat, discarded as I watched him go. I caught sight of a figure in the window of the house next door. It took me a moment to process the fact that it was a man and he was staring at me. Jack was already half way up the walkway to Slinger's house. The recess bell rang making me jump. I was alone in the alley and could feel the stranger's eyes on me as I walked down the lane. If my next door neighbor was killed would I sit at my window and watch with suspicion anyone walking down my alley? Yup, I probably would.

It wasn't until I climbed my stairs and put the key in the lock that I understood why Jack was acting so police-like. From his point of view, I was a suspect. My alibi was unsubstantiated and he'd caught me snooping around the scene of the crime. I headed to my studio, at least there things made sense.

The studio is really the second bedroom at the back of the house off the kitchen, my father's room when he was a boy. I changed it by making the window onto the backyard larger and dropping in two skylights so that even on a gloomy day it is bright. For the days when the sun does shine too brightly, the skylights had built in blinds that diffused the glare. Today I looked around at the stack of canvases, pots of paint, two large standing easels and a tabletop one. In the corner was a large metal file cabinet that doubled as a paint cupboard and held inspiration photos. In the bottom drawer were my business papers. Today I didn't feel like painting but I was restless.

"Fine," I said aloud, "Cleaning day!" I rolled up my sleeves and cleaned paint smears off the walls and floor all the while cursing the fact that I'm a very messy artist. Built in racks under the window is where I store my extra canvases, some raw, some gessoed, some with background colors and a fourth pile of rejected pieces. I cleared out the racks and looked at each canvas paying particular attention to the last pile making new decisions about what to keep, what to think about and what to sell. On the other three walls hung my finished works waiting for varnish. I checked the dates and made notes on frame sizes I needed and threw out some brushes that were dried with old paint. I took the drawers out of the cabinet and discarded wrinkled tubes and empty tubs of paint. I found paperclips, my favorite acrylic pen missing for ages and a stack of bills for cat food. That's where I stopped. I don't even own a cat. Almost a year ago, I'd given up trying to find suitable leftovers for a cat that wandered by from time to time. I called him Tom and began buying boxes of cat biscuits to give him a handful whenever our paths crossed. I kept the receipts in the drawer intending to use them as a business expense, however dubious. Was Tom Frank Slinger's overweight cat? The one Tessa told me about? I shrugged and made myself a cup of tea, sorting the bills into order while I sipped it. The rest of the day I continued my cleaning and organizing. It was dark by the time I finished and I was exhausted. The room looked spectacular, all fresh and gleaming and ready for work. I ran a hot bath, ate dinner and fell into bed.

It was still dark when I woke with a start. There was a murder in progress on my back porch, cat murder. I raced to save whoever needed saving. By the time I got there, all was quiet, Tom was licking his paw, a picture of innocence. It was clear that Tom could take care of himself. The bowl was empty so I poured in some milk. He ignored it, as cats do. I knew he'd lap it up as soon as my back was turned. I went back to bed.

I woke to scratching at the back door, I'll never get any sleep, I grumbled. It was only just starting to get light as I opened the door. Tom sidled in, casually walking past me. Half asleep, I followed him down the hall to the living room and watched him jump up to the ottoman, turn three times and lay down. Cats are like that, they know the perfect place for a nap. I was too tired to wrestle him out the door and so I went back to bed and slept heavily for another hour, waking more refreshed. I pulled on my oldest jeans and painting shirt, slid my feet into slippers and went to check on Tom. He was where I left him, the picture of contentment.

CHAPTER 6

I made coffee and stood gazing at the big cherry tree in my backyard. It was all stick arms, plain and gangly. Soon it would be transformed. I visualized the unfurling of spring leaves so vibrant the color felt alive, then flowers of palest pink crowding the tips. My daydream was interrupted by the steady drip from an overflowing gutter. Drat, first the weatherstripping and now the drains, I'd forgotten those chores. I knew from experience the eaves were clogged with cherry tree leaves. Blasted tree! It was beautiful but the leaves made a mess and my harvest was laughable, maybe a handful of cherries and a lawn full of bird spitted pits. I made a mental note to try to find a handyman who could do the work for me.

I wasn't surprised when Tom wandered into the kitchen looking very much in need of a coffee. His fur was matted and one ear was tucked. I smiled, I couldn't be angry with him for disturbing my slumber when he looked so bedraggled. He stopped in the middle of the kitchen and stared at the door. Obeying his unspoken command I opened it. He slithered down the stairs and into the hedge. I called after him, "Well sleepyhead, let me know when you want breakfast," and turned back to go in the house.

"Now would be good." Sommerville's baritone called from the back lane. He sauntered through the gate and up the sidewalk waiting at the bottom of the stairs. He smiled up at me, shrugging his shoulders and looking around, "Did you mean me?"
I just stared. He looked great, unlike me. He had on a jacket of some sort of waxed rainproof fabric and slim jeans that were tucked into dark grey Doc Marten boots. Besides what I was wearing my hair was a mess and my intention of putting on makeup everyday was already ancient history. Life isn't fair I wanted to scream. I lifted my chin, what does it matter

what a suspect wears?   It was no use, I did care. Meanwhile he stood, grinning up at me, looking like a 10-year-old waiting for a cookie, impossible to ignore.

"Hello, Inspector. If you need to talk to me you really should make an appointment," I knew I sounded peevish but that's how I felt.

He heard my tone and was contrite, "I'm sorry, you're right. It's just that investigations move fast.   If you let me know when's a good time, I can come back, Miss Stevens."

Suddenly it was too much trouble to keep my temper simmering, I was being childish and he and I both knew it. I smiled back, "Sorry, I'm being grouchy. Now is fine." I turned to go back inside,   "Would you like a coffee?"

"Sure," he said and bounded up the stairs. "I really am sorry to intrude so early. I've been up for hours so I sort of expect everyone else to be as well," he said apologetically.

"Usually I am too but I had a busy night." I shrugged.

He raised an eyebrow but I didn't feel like explaining. Let him think I was the party animal, not my roguish cat friend. "There's a hook for your coat on the porch just behind you."

He pulled it off and brushed his boots on the mat before he came through the door.   He ran his fingers through his hair, tucking a few stray curls behind his ears.

Watching him, I smoothed my own hair behind my ears. Not stopping to think first, I asked, "Doesn't the force take a dim view of inspectors with ponytails?"

He looked amused.   "So far they haven't said anything. I grew it when I was undercover a few years ago and now I just find it easier than getting regular haircuts. Basically I'm lazy."

I held his gaze then had a vague memory, oh, yeah, right, coffee. My brain slowly clicked into working order, so I turned and reached for the beans. The grinding was loud enough to keep me quiet. I assembled cups, milk and my French press and turned to find him standing at the door to my studio looking in.

As an artist I know that people want to see where I work. Mostly they only enter by invitation but that is because it is usually so messy I'm embarrassed to show it off. Today, after it's thorough cleaning it looked wonderful.

Still I hesitated, I wasn't ready for him to view my work, somehow it felt too personal. He wasn't a potential client after all. I decided he'd seen enough, "Pull up a pew," I said and placed the coffee on the table.

He looked around the kitchen. The room looked nice, all sunny and warm. He brushed his hand along the well worn wooden back of the bench, rubbed to silky smoothness by hundreds of hands over the years, "It really is a church pew," he marvelled.

"Yup, its real and it weighs a ton."

"I like it. It suits the room."

He was right. Even the grey weather couldn't dampen the glow from the rich golden walls and cupboards. And the warmth wasn't all coming from the heating vent.

He cradled the cup in his hands. "This is very good," he said.

"I've got a thing about good coffee."

"Me too, but I end up drinking too much of the bad stuff. Goes with the territory."

We were both more relaxed. Maybe it was because we were in my kitchen and not a damp and cold back lane.

I asked, "Yesterday I got the impression you considered me a suspect. Was I right?"

He said slowly, "Everyone is a suspect at the beginning of the case and you must admit your alibi was lame."

"But I'm not anymore?"

He shook his head.

"Why?"

"During the relevant time, your next door neighbour saw you a couple of times, she says she even waived at you and asked about whether it was garbage or recycling the next day."

Of course. Relief flooded through me, I hadn't realized just how much the thought of being a suspect was unsettling me. I took a sip of coffee, suddenly frivolous, "So what's on your agenda today? Cars or nosy neighbors?"
He looked at me as though I had lost my mind, "What are you talking about?"

I laughed, "Nothing just a bad night and not enough coffee. What can I do for you Inspector Sommerville?"

"This isn't an official visit, or not entirely. And you can call me Jack."

I could feel myself blushing and let out my breath slowly, "Not Jackson?"

He smiled, "The only person who calls me Jackson is my mother and then only when she's mad. As in, "Jackson, stop trying to paint the dog!"

I laughed, "Really? You're an artist?"

"Not that kind!" His impish grin made my toes curl. "I was 6 and wanted to be a fireman. That meant Barney, my black lab, had to be a Dalmatian so I decided to paint some spots on him. Barney was all for the transformation. It was Mom who took issue with it." He grinned at me like the small mischievous child he had been. "Anyway now everyone calls me Jack except my boss, who, come to think of it, is a lot like my Mom.'

Interesting, he was definitely interesting and funny, and increasingly very dangerous to my equilibrium.
I stared into my cup, "Ok Jack it is and you can call me Amy."

"Thank you Amy," he said making it sound intimate, sexy and sweet. I gulped.

"Did you say something about breakfast?" he asked.

I was having trouble concentrating. Breakfast? Who wants to eat at a time like this? Then I remembered, "I was talking to Tom,"

He looked bewildered.

"Tom is the local scrounging cat, I was offering him breakfast but never mind, its nothing. Let's make a deal. I'll make you a breakfast smoothie if you answer some questions."

I could swear he winked, "What kind of smoothie?"

This is fun, serious negotiations were in order. Hum, I what did I have on hand? "Yogurt, kale, frozen blueberries." I offered.

He considered it carefully, "if you put in a scoop of peanut butter, it's a deal"

"Peanut butter? Really? "

He nodded, "Protein."

I considered it, "Sounds interesting. So we have a deal?"

"Sure," he smiled. A shock, an electric current going at the speed of light was bouncing around my body even though I was rooted to the spot. I unplugged myself from his gaze and turned to the sink, gripping it for support.

"Do you mind if I have a look at your studio?" he asked.

I took a deep breath, "Sure, go ahead." Now that he asked, I found it wasn't a problem for me. I watched him out of the corner of my eye while I made the smoothies. He was serious and deliberate, stopping to gaze closely at each of the hanging paintings then moving on to the next. I liked that.

He only asked one question, calling out, "Do you only paint animals?"

"No, that's just what pays the bills," I replied. It was hard to express the thrill of being able to make a living at work I loved even when it didn't fulfill all my artistic dreams.

That was as close as I was prepared to let him come to my art and me. "Come and get it!" I called.

I took a tentative sip, the peanut butter added a rich texture, "De-lish, I like it."

He nodded and took a deep gulp, "Fantastic!"

I glowed.   We sat at the kitchen table in silence. Weak sunshine was streaming through the window. There was a cat was scratching at the door.

Jack lifted one eyebrow, "Is that your cat?"

Cat?   What cat?   That cat, oh yeah, Tom. I gave myself a shake while I stood up to let him in. "No. Well yes, sort of. I mean. This is Tom. He's the scrounge I mentioned. Normally I only see him every couple of weeks." I bent to give his head a rub, "In the past couple of days he seems to have decided to make this his second home."

Jack studied Tom as the cat slid across the floor and padded up to the fridge where he stopped to lick one paw, "You know what?   He looks a lot like Smooch, in fact I'm sure it's the same cat."

I burst out laughing, "Smooch! You must be kidding! Who names their cat Smooch?"

He replied slowly watching me, "Frank Slinger."
A wave of sorrow came over me.   It must have shown on my face, "Oh, how sad."

"What's sad about it?"

"Don't you think it would be fun to know someone, particularly a man, who calls his cat, Smooch.   I wish I'd known Frank Slinger."

Jack was silent. We sat in the sunshine and regarded the cat as he sniffed the fridge.

I got up, "Well Tom Smooch, you're all alone aren't you?" I bent to stroke his fur then opened the fridge and gave him a bit of left over chicken.

oNe WORD

CHAPTER 7

Smooch licked his paws after his mid-morning treat and curled up on the heat vent under the table. While it felt companionable and cozy it was an illusion. It was time to find out why there was a policeman in my kitchen. I turned to Jack and asked abruptly, "Why did you come here today?"

"You had some questions, " he replied and finished his smoothy in one gulp. "Go ahead and ask," he smiled, "then I'll ask mine."

"Don't make it easy do you?" I replied grinning, "That's ok, I like a challenge."
I thought for a moment, "Ok, first, how did he die?"

Sommerville hesitated answering carefully, "For now, I'll just say that it was murder and it wasn't random."

"No other details?"

"No, not that I can share."

Bummer, details are what I wanted. "Well, who discovered the body?"

"An anonymous phone call, male."

This was going nowhere fast. I tried again, "What time did he die?"

"You know the answer to that, between 3 and 7"

"No, I mean exactly. Can't you narrow it down?"

"No."

I was sure there was a more precise time frame. I regarded him sceptically, "Ok, I'm done."

He was surprised. "That's it? I thought you had more questions."

"I do but if you're going to avoid them, even the easy ones, I'll just have to find the answers some other way." I smiled sweetly thinking of Tessa. "So your questions?"

He looked at me suspiciously, then became serious, "Well, the first is the same as before, do you remember what you saw or heard that night?"

I tried to look as innocent, "If I had a better idea of the time I might be able to jog my memory but..." I shrugged leaving the sentence hanging.

He narrowed his eyes guessing what I was up to, "What if I were to suggest between 530 and 6?"

I smiled brightly, "Doesn't ring any bells but I promise to think about it!"

His next question surprised me, "Who in your group would be considered an expert knitter?"

"You're asking about my knitting group?"

"Yes."

"Seriously?"

He nodded.

"Well, it depends. Of the group you met the other night, I'd say Minnie is the most experienced, I mean if you are asking in terms of number of finished pieces. She knits for charity and churns out an incredible number of hats, booties and blankets. They are all based on the same pattern though. I doubt she could design or even alter a pattern. I don't know too much about Mariko because she has only been coming for a couple of months and so far she only knits doll clothes. She is obviously very careful and her finished pieces are beautiful but I don't know if she can knit a full sized garment or not. Jen and George come more for the snacks and chat. I know they can both knit as I have seen them make hats and touques but I don't think either has made anything very complicated. Tessa is the wild child. She designs all her own patterns, mixes and matches yarns and other stuff. On the other hand not too long ago she said she had never done a cable, which is a pretty basic stitch. So I would call Tessa an expert of design, not of actual knitting technique. For example, she once made a hat out of yarn and pieces of tin foil."

Sommerville laughed.

"It really was astounding. She only stopped wearing it when someone mentioned the possibility of being struck by lightning." I grinned at the memory. "The only members of the group that you haven't met are Claire, who is a beginner, and Meg. In terms of skill level, Meg is the most expert. She's in Paris for a year working."

He shook his head, "What about you?"

I thought about it for a minute, "I knit a lot. I design patterns and even sell some of them. Even so I find there is always something new to learn."

"Still you'd probably be the most all around expert of the group?"

"Except for Meg, I guess so. It really depends on why you need to know."

MINNIE, TESSA, MARIKO, JEN, GEORGE,
CLAIRE, MEG, AMY

"I have to check a few things first before I can tell you why. Second question. Can I have a look at your basement?"

I was dumbfounded. "Now?"

He nodded.

"The only entrance is outside. You really want to do this now?"

"Yes," he said. I just stared at him while he settled back in the bench crossing his long legs and showing off his Doc Martins. They were well worn and clearly well cared for; no icy salt marks marred the finish.

"Not unless you tell me why," I said stubbornly.

"I will, just let me have a look." My eyes must have shown my skepticism. He added, "I promise."

Shaking my head, I turned down the hall to take my coat off the hook by the front door.

As I came back I said, "Ok, if you insist. Grab your coat. It's cold down there."

Tom Smooch was rubbing against the door. He followed us down the stairs.

"Tell me about the house," Jack requested.

I had no idea why he wanted to know but decided to humor him. "Well, my Grandfather built it in 1953. That's what he did for a living, building houses. I understand it was a popular design. Later he started making larger homes by taking the same basic design and adding a second floor. This one was just for him and grandma and their son, my father. The size of the house wasn't important to him, he cared more about having enough space for his vegetable garden. The raised beds are still back there, under the leaves and his favorite cherry tree which shades the back of the house in summer."

cap S

I stepped over the basement's raised threshold, built to keep out water and debris and a perfect place for a deadly trip. "Watch your step."

"Was Grandpa a midget?" Jack asked as he eyed the beams that lowered the ceiling in some places to just over five foot.

FEET.

"No, he was almost 6 foot and must have hit his head a million times, I know I did."

FEET

Jack dodged the large structural beam running the length of the house.
I pointed at it, "I call that one T-Rex; it's an attack beam."

"It looks lethal. Is that why you have foam taped over the edges?" he laughed.

"I can't tell you how many times I banged my head. Since I put up the foam I haven't hit it once." I grinned. "I always wondered why Grandpa didn't dig a bit deeper and make it full height."

"Maybe it had to do with zoning or taxes."

"You may be right. I never thought of it except that Grandpa was very careful about money. He made a lot and lost it all a couple of times over the years. My guess is that the height just didn't matter. To Grandpa it was simply a cold storage and laundry room for Grandma. She was short so the ceiling height wasn't a problem. I remember barrels of pickles, jars of fruit, jellies and jams and wooden crates stuffed with straw and homegrown carrots, turnips and potatoes. "

He looked around, "And there?" he pointed at a small door.

I led him to the area under the front stairs opening the door. "This is the cold-er cold storage. He stored his homemade blackberry wine here."

"Was it any good?" Jack asked.

"If I tell you that he served it mixed with seven-up, does that tell you?"

He looked into the dark hole, "Wine all gone? You don't have any left? What if it just needed aging?"

"Actually I hate to admit it but with the seven-up it wasn't bad at all. He was way ahead of his time, making wine spritzers. Sadly no, it's all gone."

The cold storage was dark, clean and now held my own jars of pickles, pears, peaches and jams.   Jack pointed, "Grandma's?"

"Mine," I couldn't keep the pride out of my voice. "When I bought the place 5 years ago it was rented for years and there was nothing left of my Grandparents except some tools and the old mangle."   GRANDPARENT'S

I led the way to the far corner.   "Here is Grandfather's workbench. The renters left the basement pretty much alone so when I bought it I inherited his tools and gardening stuff. And this is the laundry area." I waved a hand at the machines.

He fingered the mangle, "Do you use this?"

"No, I tried but it wrinkled everything and I hate ironing. It's still here because it's too heavy to move and no one wants it anyway."

I said a silent prayer of thanks that this wasn't one of the days my underwear dripped from the drying lines in the basement. I'd been embarrassed enough.

"What's this?" He pointed to a metal shaft near the centre of the room.

"That's the laundry chute. I think originally it was something for getting the coal or ashes from the big kitchen range, the source of heat and cooking in the old days. The stove was long gone when I got the place. All that was left was the panel door and chute so I had it rerouted to the bathroom for laundry."

We stood and stared while Tom Smooch climbed into the laundry basket, kneading the dirty towel in it. Circling, he settled down for a nap. Finally I asked, "That's my part of the bargain. What's this all about?"

"I think your Grandfather must have built Slinger's house as well. It's very similar. Slinger was something of a packrat and between his stuff, a load of boxes full of papers and the forensics crew I can't get a really good look around yet. I like to get a feel for the surroundings when I am investigating and when I was here before I guessed that your house was similar to Slinger's."

Now that he mentioned it, I knew he was right. Slinger's house model had the second floor. That made it look more substantial and over the years it was also updated. The front porch was enclosed in glass, a wonderful improvement in our damp climate even though it changed the old-style character of the house. It certainly changed Slinger's house, "I never guessed it was one of Grandpa's houses."

"Even down to the basement for Minions," he grinned.

"I never asked Grandfather which houses he built, I just assumed they were all over the city. I like the idea that many of the homes right here are his. I'll have to see if I can get more information someday," I paused, "I'd love to see inside Slinger's house."

"I suppose after all this is over it might be possible," he said as we turned to leave. He motioned to the cat sleeping peacefully in the laundry, "What about Smooch?"

"Oh there's a cat door on the side of the house. He knows where it is, he used it the other night."

"Show me."

"It's easier to see from the outside."

So we trudged around the outside. There was a storm door about 2 foot square bolted to the house locked from the inside. Cut into it was a small door on a hinge. "It only works one way, to get out of the basement. I really don't want Tom or anything else coming and going without my knowing it. "

"Slinger doesn't have one of these. You said the cat used it one night recently. Which night was it?"

COMMA, NOT PERIOD

"Oh. It must have been knit night. Just before everyone arrived I came down to get a jar of strawberry jam and Tom followed me in. He was busy exploring so I left him to it and went upstairs."

Jack looked thoughtful and as I turned to head back up the stairs he rested his hand on my sleeve, "I have to go back to the station but I'll be in touch. Thanks for the tour."

"I hope it helped," I watched him walk to the lane my arm still warm from his touch. Get a grip I told myself crossly, you're acting like a teenager.

Over another cup of coffee, I forced the thought of Jack aside to concentrate on something almost as interesting, murder. It was so unreal. I wasn't sad or frightened; I was curious. Frank Slinger was unknown to me and yet a close neighbor. And his murder had nothing to do with me. Nevertheless I was caught inside, like an extra in a movie, not part of but on the periphery of the action.

I considered the problem. What did I know? Our houses were similar, Slinger was a pack rat, he owned an overweight cat with a cute name and his death had something to do with knitting. Actually Jack hadn't told me that but I felt it was a good guess. Truthfully he hadn't told me anything, except that it was murder.

Tessa, George and Jen all called later in the day. The neighborhood was buzzing. I reported what I knew. They were all interested to hear it was murder. Without any details there was nothing I could add. Tessa did say that her cleaning lady, Rose, who she shared with Jen and George cleaned for a bunch of people in the neighborhood. On the theory that cleaning ladies know everything, Tessa promised to ask Rose what she knew and report back. *add the U*

The local paper wasn't out till the next day. Jen laughed when I suggested she get back on staff immediately. The TV evening news did have a short story about the death. The picture they showed was the same guy I remembered from Tessa's description. He didn't look sinister. In fact he looked dull and boring. He was the retired manager of the local postal sorting station, a member of the historical committee and did drive for cancer. So far Tessa was proving a good detective. Then Jack came on the screen. I shouldn't have been surprised to see him, it was a standard procedure. He looked capable and gorgeous as he confirmed that it was murder and gave a phone number for the tip line. That was a mistake I thought, smiling. Giving out his number would probably produce a flood/phone calls from lovelorn ladies with doubtful information. I grinned as I briefly considered leaving mine. Anonymously, of course.

CHAPTER 8

Even though the murder was the most interesting thing to ever happen in the neighborhood I reminded myself that it was nothing to do with me. I was finding it too distracting. I needed to get to work and pay some bills. That is one disadvantage of working from home; it's too easy to be lead astray.

After the cleaning, my studio felt lighter and airier. I looked around the room and felt proud of the work that hung on the walls and grateful that I was so content. It had taken me a long time to get to this place in mind and body and that alone made it special. I pulled on a painting apron and stood back to consider the canvas propped on my easel.

I make my living by painting portraits of animals, usually pets. Like most jobs I fell into it gradually and keep at it because it pays the bills and I enjoy it. The first pet portrait I'd done was of my bunny, Whiskers. Whiskers was white and fluffy and I was 8. I remember trying to capture his downy fur on canvas with a toothbrush. It took ages and didn't come out as I wanted. It hung in my bedroom for years. Then one day it disappeared under a Smashing Pumpkins poster.

As I was growing up I made art, like other kids made mud pies, messy and fun but never taking it seriously. When I left school I did a bunch of boring jobs, wandering through the workforce. Then I got a summer job as a camp counsellor and ended up running the craft station. It rained all summer and so I was busy. It was a blast, the best part was learning the joy of painting again. Later I stayed on as a staff coordinator for the camp and with more time on my hands bought some supplies and looked around for something to paint. My aunt suggested her Siamese cat. I tried painting Sukey as a live model. That was the first and last time I used live animal models, what on earth was I thinking? Instead I took a camera to my aunt's house and took dozens of shots of the cat sleeping, stretching, and playing. My aunt picked out the three she liked best and I used them to compose a portrait of Sukey staring right at the viewer with her startling blue eyes and just the hint of what looked like a smile. My Aunt was delighted and hung it in her living room. That was enough for me to get two more commissions from her friends. After a few years I was able to quit the camp. I'll never be rich but to be able to work at something I love and pay the bills was intensely gratifying.

Today I was considering the yellow ringed eyes of an iguana. No matter how hard I tried I could not see any expression in Sid. Beth, his owner, adored him and the pose she asked for was one with her hand feeding Fred a piece of apple. The hand and fruit were no problem; even Fred looked good, all rough wrinkles. But it lacked my pizazz.

My pet portraits are distinctive because I paint the expression that most captures the animal's personality, or at least what the owner thinks is their personality. I could get nothing out of Sid but boredom. His owner was besotted with him and giggled saying he was a little devil, always playing tricks. Iguana tricks? I didn't ask.

A lot of painting is staring at the canvas willing it to tell you what needs to be done. With chalk I made various scribbles and bushed them off. Eventually I mixed some Naples yellow and Prussian blue and put a tiny crescent shaped dab in the corner of his black eye. I smiled, it was perfect he looked a bit shifty. I spent a little more time laying in textures in the background until I was happy with the effect. Done. I hung it on the wall to let it dry and also so that I could continue to consider it from time to time.

I stretched deciding what to work on next. I had just landed a contract to do a series of paintings for a local organic pet food manufacturer. They wanted 12 different animals for a calendar. In payment they offered me a load of pet food. When they learned I don't own a pet we came to terms.

That surprises all my clients, the fact that I don't have a pet. My stock answer is to laugh and remind people that I spend every day with pets. But the real reason is that I've never gotten over Whiskers. Bunnies are the best. I was positive of this at 8 and still love them. When Whiskers developed some sort of rash and slowly lost all his gorgeous white fur, I was heartbroken. No more pets I decided then and so far I'd stuck to that rule. So what about Tom Smooch? He was no trouble but did I really want the responsibility? I decided it would be cruel to ignore him, especially now. I was cornered. Then I brightened, maybe Minnie wanted a cat.

Thinking of Minnie reminded me I still hadn't seen or spoken to her since knit night. I decided to give her a call. There was no answer. Out again? How strange. Minnie doesn't have an answering machine or a cell phone. When asked she replies, "Why do I need one of those, I'm always home." And the idea of Minnie on a computer is laughable. I decided to try again later and went to make a cup of tea.

I couldn't get Slinger out of my mind. It's funny how when something dramatic happens you feel involved. I wanted to help in some way, Mr. Slinger sounded like a nice man and to be murdered was horrible. I sipped my tea and looked through the local newspaper. There were the usual grocery ads, pictures of school kids doing amazing things and notices of city council doing nothing. There was a short news story on the murder with even fewer details than I knew. At the back, Slinger's name popped out of the page. There was to be a memorial service the following day. I never pay attention to obits however this one sounded strange even to me. It read,

"The church of St. Cuthbert will host a memorial service for Frank Slinger, our loyal parishioner.   3pm Sunday, light refreshments in the church hall following."

It was terse.   Did they really expect anyone to show up at such short notice?   It was also a little odd that the church itself seemed to be the host.   And "Loyal Parishioner,"   did that mean that he volunteered at the church?   He seemed a nice guy so that was likely or the more cynical me wondered if he was a big donor?

I mentioned it to Tessa when she called.

"Shall we go?" she asked.

"I don't know.   Do you think anyone else will be there? I mean it doesn't sound like he has any family or anything. And it seems so quick, even if there are relatives how could they have organized anything this quickly?"

"It's not a funeral, just a memorial service and the church people must be interested or they wouldn't be hosting it."

Still I hesitated, "And a Sunday.   Who holds a memorial service on a Sunday? Don't you think that's a little weird?"

Tessa was practical, "Well let's go find out."

"I don't know, " I hesitated then smiled reminding her of a favourite movie scene. "I don't want to be like Audrey Hepburn in "Charade". You know when it's just her and her friend with the cop at the back cleaning his nails," I laughed.

Tess got the reference immediately. She giggled, "You do too want to be Audrey Hepburn!"

I gave in, "You are soooo right. Seriously though, he does sound like a good person and for that reason I'll go. Anyway, I have nothing else to do on Sunday afternoon."

"And maybe Cary Grant will show up," Tessa teased as she rang off.

The light held long enough for me to block out a sketch for the calendar. I was quite looking forward to 12 different portraits and the best news was that the company was giving me the freedom to choose the animals and an easy deadline so I could take my time. The only restriction they made was that the animals must be 'proper pets'. I read between the lines realizing they only wanted animals who ate their pet food, of course. I decided to start with May and a delightful pair of cuddling budgies. I worked steadily for the remainder of the day alternately trying to connect with Minnie by phone, worrying about her, and getting lost in the paint.

Normally I see Minnie every couple of days. Often we go shopping together. Because she cooks for her live-in student she needs a lot of groceries and I'm happy to go with her and haul bags. Otherwise she is always at home. Minnie spends the better part of her day on the phone. She loves the telephone. She sits in her big armchair, puts her feet up, hits speakerphone and knits while chatting to her large circle of friends.

By evening I had tried to reach Minnie four times, this was the fifth. She picked up on the sixth ring, "Hello?" she said timidly.

"Minnie, what on earth is wrong?" When she didn't reply I carried on, "Where have you been? I've been worried."

There was a long pause before she replied with a tremor in her voice, "It's nothing."

"Minnie, it can't be 'nothing'. I've tried calling you all day! You looked ill on knit night."

"I'm fine, I just don't want to talk about it. Please!" she pleaded.

I was shocked. I'd never heard her so stricken, "Minnie, I'm coming over."

"No don't do that ! Please Amy! I just need to... I have a ... it's just that that man died and he was a bully and I am glad he died and.." her voice trailed off.

"Slinger? He was a bully? Why do you say that?"

"I know I shouldn't." She stammered, "It's awful. It's all over now anyway. I'm so ashamed."

"Minnie, you're not making any sense. What could you possibly have to be ashamed of?"

She blurted out, "Yes, I mean no. Oh Amy, I'm glad he's dead! That's why I'm so ashamed, I'm just so relieved."

It was hard to think of something to say, "Minnie, calm down. I'll be right over. We can work this out," I said, even though I wasn't at all sure that was the case.

"No," she said forcefully. In a calmer voice she continued, "No Amy, please don't come over. I'm fine really. It has been a shock but I'm better. I promise that I will see you soon, just not right now."

"Are you sure?" I questioned.

"Yes I am. I have to go, Mariko is here. I'm fine. Really," she said and hung up.

I sat staring at the phone before finally ending the call. Minnie was the least complicated person I knew. This was so out of character for her. Should I ignore her request and go over to see her? There are times when you should ignore the words and follow your gut. I decided this wasn't one of them. Minnie was a grown woman, if she said she didn't want to see me then I would have to accept that. Knowing Mariko was with her made me feel a lot better. Tomorrow, all bets are off. Tomorrow I won't ask, I'll just show up.

CHAPTER 9

Sunday was warm and drier. It looked like the sun might even peek through. It was a good day for a memorial service but I was having second thoughts about attending the ceremony. What kind of man was the real Frank Slinger? He was a volunteer driver for the cancer clinic but according to Minnie he was also a bully. Was that possible? Can bullies do good things? Sure I decided, cynically, if it's in their own interests.

Did I trust Minnie's judgement? Yes. If she said Slinger was no good then I believed her. She is no fool even though normally she looks like a fluffy kitten.

I admire Minnie. After her husband died she made a full life for herself and that included clawing her way out of the financial crunch he left her in. She was kind and generous and for her to call Slinger a bully meant that he must have been really evil. Anything less and Minnie would have been more forgiving.

Since my reason for going to the service was based on the idea that he was a nice guy I had a re-think. I tried to call Tessa to cancel our plans but there was no answer and she didn't respond to my text. It was getting late, reluctantly I grabbed my coat and headed down the street, silently cursing people who have cell phones and don't respond to calls, messages and texts and people who don't have cell phones at all.

It was a lovely day and the walk did me good. By the time I got to the church I was no longer annoyed. I spotted Tessa immediately. What is she wearing? It looked a little strange for a funeral, a navy pea coat with gathered netting in the palest pink sewn all around the hem, edge and collar.

She caught me staring, "Isn't it darling? It took me forever to find the right shade of tulle!"

Actually it was adorable, she looked warm and snug and feminine. How does she do it? I asked myself for the hundredth time. "I guess there's no pocket for your cell?" I asked still miffed.

"What do you mean?" she said as she pulled out her phone. Seeing the missed call and text, she was apologetic, "Oh. Sorry. What were you calling about?"

"Never mind, we're here now."

She scanned my outfit and muttered, "We have to go shopping."

I knew she was right. Because I'd decided at the last minute to come my outfit was items grabbed at random. At best I looked unremarkable, at worst, boring. While I was content with my life; a job I love, a home that is comfortable and enough money to indulge in travel, I was a little less satisfied with my look. Overall I knew I was a bit of a mess, except for my shoes. I love shoes. I keep them in their own boxes, I polish them, I have them mended. I look after them and they look after me.

Tessa and I sat at the end of a pew in the middle of the church. I looked down at my feet and admired my flats. A deep burgundy patent leather, they had zippers sewn diagonally across the pointed toes. Tessa could help me with my clothes but she'd have to leave my shoes alone, I thought stubbornly.

A pair of oxblood tasselled slip-ons stood in the aisle next to me. I didn't look up, I didn't need to, the Inspector was here and he wore beautiful shoes.

"May I join you?" Jack's velvet whisper enveloped us.

"Un huh," I muttered as I tried to shuffle Tessa down the pew. Tessa wasn't cooperating, she wouldn't budge. Jack sat in the very little space at the end of the pew so close to me I could see the stubble patch he missed shaving that morning. My arm, where it touched his, was on fire. I elbowed Tessa. With a smirk and rubbing her side she slid a further 2 inches down the pew. I could breathe again.

Other than our whispered greeting it was quiet in the church. Soft music began playing in the background, canned but calming. Slowly I willed myself to relax, my eyes fixated on his shoes. They looked nice next to mine, a his and her pair like they were on a date. I shook my head, I was being ridiculous. I looked around concentrating on the church. This was the first time I'd seen it. A beautiful old building with real stained glass windows, not those awful painted ones. The pews were solid wood, like the one in my kitchen and the whole building smelled of lemon polish, it was lovely.

Before it even began the service was over. I was incredulous. It couldn't be over, could it? Start to finish it couldn't have been more than 10 minutes, probably less. No singing or eulogy. No one in the sparse congregation spoke. Even the minister confined her remarks to snippets from the Bible. Absolutely nothing of a personal nature was said about the man.

There weren't more than a couple dozen people in the church and they were pulling on hats and gloves. It really was over. I sat back shaking my head. Why had the church even bothered?

Of the few people there, the only one I knew was Minnie. I pointed her out to Tessa and whispered, "Did you know she was coming?"

"No, maybe she knew Slinger through the church," Tessa said.

The minister was announcing that refreshments were available in the hall. I looked at Jack, "Wow that was quick. What's that all about?"

"What do you think?" he asked.

"Do you never answer a simple question?"

He titled his head to the side, reminding me of Rocco, a German shepherd I'd painted. He cocked his head just like that whenever I spoke. It was adorable. Like, Rocco he just stared.

I gave up and answered him, "Well something is up. I mean the church puts out a notice saying they are honoring a valued parishioner and then provide a service that is so quick as to be disgraceful. I've been to longer memorials for a stray dog."

Neither Jack nor Tessa disagreed. We made our way to the church hall, few others did. I saw Minnie, looking grim, heading back to her car. I thought about trying to catch up to her but didn't want to drag Tessa or worse, Jack into something that Minnie didn't want anyone to know about. Jack had a worrying habit of following me around, or so it seemed. Maybe it was just that I was too attuned to his presence.

In the hall Tessa looked around, "Not much of a turnout. Maybe they know the kind of light refreshments the church generally offers." She eyed with distaste the small table with packages of instant coffee, powdered cream, sugar and plastic stir sticks. Nearby a kettle was surrounded by a jumble sale collection of mismatched mugs. The only snack was an open bag of Peak Freen cookies.

More interesting than the paltry refreshments were the few people scattered around the room. Including us and the minister there were less than a dozen people in the hall. These few must be the people closest to Slinger, I guessed.

The minister was a middle-aged woman being followed by a short ferrety man. He kept plucking at her robe, it was clear she was barely suppressing her annoyance.

An older woman clutching a string bag was surreptitiously stuffing cookies into her pockets. A man in a post office uniform held a cup of coffee but wasn't drinking. Near the entrance stood a silent couple, looking dazed. She clutched his arm as he stood stiffly looking at the floor. Another older woman in a hideous brown coat and old lace up boots was scanning the room with a look of scorn or fury or both. Anger radiated off her. Then she turned abruptly and left, jostling a man standing in the shadow of the exit. I thought I recognized him as Slinger's neighbor, the man in the window.

"The usual suspects," Jack muttered with the hint of a smile bringing me back to earth.

Briefly I was shocked at his flippancy, this was a memorial service after all. But he was right, no one was distraught, there were no tears. The one word to sum up the atmosphere was relieved. We were the epitome of a cast of characters out of a British mystery.

"All we need is a handyman. These days it isn't the butler, it's the handyman who done it" I said in a cockney whisper.

Jack stifled a laugh.

"Who are all these people?" I asked.

"Let's see. That is Jane Harper, the minister with Bob Strauss, your handyman in tow." He grinned. "Don't get any ideas thinking you've solved the case! The old lady at the cookies is Mrs. Walker, I doubt she even knew Slinger, she comes to lots of events and loads up on the free food. The couple at the entrance is Mr. and Mrs. Richter. According to the minister they worked with Slinger on the historical committee."

"What about relatives? Friends? Co-workers? Neighbors?"

"That's a co-worker," he waved in the direction of the man with the coffee cup, "Fred Birch. As you can see from the jacket he still works at the postal office."

"And the guy at the exit? He looks suspicious."

"He's Carl something. Can't remember his last name, lives next door to Slinger." He confirmed my guess. "We are still tracking down relatives."

"Sparse, I'd say. So why is the church having the service? Is it because of what he did for the church?"

"As far as I know, yes, something to do with historical archiving, I've been told."

"What kind of historical stuff does a church need?"

"No idea, you'll have to ask the minister," he turned catching sight of the Richters, murmured "back to work" and took off in their direction. Tessa had wandered off towards the refreshments. I looked around and caught the eye of the Reverend. She had succeeded in shaking off the handyman. She looked more relaxed and smiled in my direction. I made my way over, "Hello, Reverend Harper is it?"

"Yes, please call me Jane"

Tessa was talking to the cookie stealer. Was she actually helping to empty the remaining cookies into the old woman's string bag? I spoke louder than I intended hoping to divert the minister's attention, "I'm Amy. I think it's very nice that you held a service for Mr. Slinger. He sounds like a good man."

Her smile became forced. "So you didn't know him?'

"No, he was a neighbour and I just found out that my Grandfather actually built his house but I don't think I ever met him."

She was curious, "Then why are you here?"

"I don't really know, I'm interested and somehow I feel involved," I said sheepishly.

She was about to say something when handyman Bob plucked at her sleeve again, "Jane? What about the flowers, Jane?"

Provoked by the interruption she turned to him, "Bob, what is wrong with you today?" Wearily she added, "I'm sorry, I'll be with you in a minute."

She turned back to me and said, "Come another time," She looked at me shrewdly, "I'd like to have a chat." I nodded as she turned to deal with Bob's complaint.

Why did she want to talk to me? Drumming up new parishioners? I scanned the room but couldn't see Jack anywhere and it looked like Mr. and Mrs. Richter were leaving. On impulse I stepped up to them and said cheerily, "Nice service wasn't it?"

They stared at me. I tried a different tack, "I'm Amy Stevens and I've heard that you are on the historical committee." Mr.

Richter looked smug so I loaded it on, "It must be fascinating. Can you tell me what kind of work the committee does?"

"We are critical to the history of Port Oxford," Mr. Richter said pompously. "I'm in charge of all the documents. It is my job to see that we preserve the church and old city records, putting the information on computers. This church is the oldest in the area."

"That's marvellous," I gushed, "and I understand Mr. Slinger was on the committee. How did he help?"

Mr. Richter frowned, "He was no help at all."

"Oh, Oscar" his wife said plaintively.

"Well, it's true. All he ever did was take documents and then return them saying he didn't get around to doing anything with them. He was supposed to be inputting the information into our database. If I had my way I would have put him off the committee," he said with some satisfaction.

Mrs. Richter must have realized how rude her husband sounded. Embarrassed she looked around then murmured, "I know dear, and now...." She left the words hanging and blushed vividly, "oh I didn't mean..."

Mr. Richter took her by the arm. "We have to go," he declared. They hurried to the exit. It was clear that they weren't just relieved, they were delighted Slinger was dead.

It was looking like the Richters shared Minnie's assessment of Slinger. What about the Reverend? I hesitated then added Jane Harper to the list, besides I was puzzled by her invitation to me. What did any of this have to do with his murder?

CHAPTER 10

The minister and Bob were heading for the door. Tessa was hugging Mrs. Walker, the cookie monster, farewell. I couldn't see Jack anywhere. Everyone else was gone so I walked over to Tessa.

"That poor lady, she is so hungry," she said watching the retreating figure with concern.

"According to Jack, she shows up at do's all over the city, eats all the food and disappears with the leftovers."

Tessa sniffed, "What does he know?"

"He's a detective," I pointed out laughing. "Never mind about that, let's go for sushi tonight. I want to talk to you about shopping."

"Really! You want to go shopping? When?"

"I don't know, Monday or Tuesday, maybe. We can talk about it over dinner."

"Can't tonight, sorry. I have a date."

"Anyone I know?" Tessa frequently has a new man in her life, I'd long since given up trying to keep track.

"Jeff."

"Isn't he the guy fixing your stairs?"

"Yes."

"I thought you said you were never going to date another tradesman after Smith or Smurf or whatever his name was."

"Smythe. I changed my mind. He's taking me to La Table Noir."

"Is that the place where you dine completely in the dark?"

"Yes, it sounds like fun."

"Is he that bad looking?" Only Tessa would go on a first date to a restaurant where she couldn't see her partner. On second thought since he chose the place he might just be quirky enough to have potential. I wished her luck adding, "Just think, you can dump him at the restaurant and he won't even know you're gone!"

Tessa gave me an evil grin, "I know!"

We walked out to the churchyard. Tessa headed off to the car park saying she would call later to set up a shopping date. Across the lawn Jack caught my eye and motioned me to wait. He was talking with Bob who was shifting from foot to foot, staring at the ground. Jack looked irritated. Eventually Bob pulled his baseball cap down and scurried away. Jack came over shaking his head, "Sometimes I hate my job," he paused, "I wanted to ask, what was your friend doing here?"

"Who Tessa? Oh you mean Minnie. Don't know, I didn't even know she was coming. But I guess probably the same thing as Tessa and me, doing the neighborly thing." I didn't mention that her coming had surprised me and that her behavior was totally out of character.

He looked skeptical. I silently agreed with him. Why was Minnie at the service? She didn't like Slinger, she'd made that clear so why make the effort to come? And why leave so fast? She must have seen Tessa and me and yet she avoided us. Now I really needed to find out what was going on with her. Hopefully she went home directly from the service and I'd be able to catch her there.

I tried to make Minnie's appearance at the service sound normal, "People have different reasons for coming to memorials. Slinger lived just down the block from her. They may have chatted over the fence."

"Maybe." He still didn't sound convinced. We walked down the path towards the street.

"Well, the same applies of you. Why are you here?" I asked.

"In a murder investigation I usually try to go to the funeral. It's often surprising who shows up."

"Like who? The murderer?" I smiled but he was serious. "Really? I thought that only happens in books."

He shrugged, "Its common sense that the people who show up at a funeral are those who were closest to the dead person. Any of them might know something to help with the investigation." He gazed at me intently, "Like you and the memory you are having trouble recalling."

Frustrated I cried, "I wish I'd never said anything, at least not until or even if I remembered it!" By this time we had reached the street. Constable Bradley drove up, calling, "You ready to go sir?"

"Yeah." Jack turned back to me smiling, "Don't look so worried, we know you aren't a suspect."

That wasn't what was worrying me. What if, because Tessa and Minnie were at the service, that made them potential suspects? The idea was ludicrous. I felt sure that both were innocent even as doubt about Minnie edged its way into my brain.

My thoughts were dark as I walked home. The trees lining the road are so old and dense that even without their leaves they look full. Weak sunshine filtering through the branches made stark graphic patterns on the road. It was unsettling, matching my mood.

I faced the fact that Minnie's distress must be linked to Slinger's death. She had been fine at knit night until the first mention of police. It was only after Tessa mentioned the patrol car in the street that she paled and became uneasy. She had to be connected but in what way I had no idea.

Since any lingering sympathy I had for Slinger was gone, his murder was now simply a puzzle. I love solving puzzles, especially mysteries. Maybe the answer would even help Minnie. Encouraged, I imagined if I were the police where would I start? With MOM, of course, I laughed aloud. Motive, Opportunity and Means.

First, motive. Why are people murdered? Random, revenge, money I couldn't think of anything else. Given the little I knew about Slinger was it possible for me to work out a motive?

I ticked them off. Random? Jack told me it wasn't random. Good, one down!

How about revenge? That was a possibility. Revenge for what? Jealousy, hatred ? I had no idea, it could be any of a million reasons. Leave that one on the table.

Money? Too much or too little? He certainly wasn't flashing it around. Both his house and the collector car were worth a fair amount but they were also things he must have owned for many years. So that answered both sides of that question. Of course he could have a treasure chest of diamonds or a desk stuffed with IOUs for all I knew.

That did raise another possibility, could it be theft gone wrong? No, surely that would be considered random by the police. Unless it was theft by someone he knew. That might fit. So what was worth stealing? The car was still in the garage and it was too valuable not to be a target. Was anything else missing from his home? Jack hadn't said specifically. He did mention that the place was overcrowded with stuff and it would have been natural for him to add that the mess was a result of a thief ransacking the place. But he didn't and somehow I thought he would have. So robbery as a motive didn't seem likely.

There was always sex. That was another motive I'd forgotten. Was there a disgruntled ex or partner in the picture? If there was then they should have been at the service. Looking back nobody fit that description. There was always paid sex. Maybe Slinger was a pimp and his house was a brothel; this was absurd, I knew too little to speculate properly.

Anyone peeking out their curtains must have thought I was insane, muttering and laughing to myself as I walked up the quiet street. I gave up. I hadn't gotten very far with a possible motive and I had no idea as to opportunity or means. It was like trying to put together a jigsaw with 3/4 of the pieces missing.

Meanwhile there was Minnie to think about. The bubbly happy Minnie I loved was gone, replaced by a fragile old woman. She looked like she had shrunk. Since my dinner plans with Tessa were a bust I diverted back to my house and got a pot of soup out of the freezer and loaded it into the trunk of the car. Food first then answers, I planned. I drove over and pulled up in front of Minnie's house just as Mariko rounded the street corner. I got out of the car as she ran up. "What is wrong?" She asked, glancing at the house.

I was startled, "Mariko, what do you mean? Why would something be wrong?"

Leaving the soup in the trunk I put my arm around her. "Tell me," I said walking with her slowly up the sidewalk.

I couldn't see her face, the dark veil of hair sheltered her eyes. She spoke softly, choosing her words, "Minnie. She is not happy."

"Mariko, I know," I agreed. "Is she home now?"

"Maybe. Sometimes she is out. She never before. Now. Maybe"

"Before? How long before?" Mariko just stared at me uncomprehending. "Sorry, do you mean she's been different lately? Even before Knit night? " Mariko nodded. "How long has she been different?"

"Not long after I come. Some weeks wonderful then wrong and now worse."

We were on the front porch. Mariko took out her key and let us in, calling out for Minnie. There was no answer. Mariko took off her coat and hung it in the closet, I kept mine on, declining when Mariko offered to make tea.

"I'll come back when Minnie is home. Meanwhile tell me what is wrong, or different, what's worrying you."

"Everything," she said simply. "Before she make laundry Tuesday. I know and remember to give. Now she does other days, I not know."

"Well, that is a little odd but not something to worry about," I smiled gently.

Mariko was unconvinced, "Also the cooking."

"Cooking?"

"She cook and cook. I do not see the food."

"What do you mean?" I asked bewildered.

"Last week she make that noodle dish with tomato and spinach, the one that has 'g' you don't say."

It took me a minute to figure out what she meant, "Lasagna?"

"Yes! Minnie's very good and she knows I love it. She makes a big pan and I am happy. I think I will have lots. The next day I look and it is gone."

"Maybe she just put it in the freezer?"

"No. It has gone. I am worried, she is different. She is very nice and kind," Mariko frowned, "but now she is all the time in her room and not come out."

I wasn't too concerned about the laundry or lasagna but for Minnie to stay in her room, that was very strange. Minnie is so sociable. I tried to reassure Mariko, "I'll talk with her and find out what is going on. "

"Okay," Mariko said doubtfully.

I laid my hand on her arm, "Mariko, I promise. When you see her tell her she must come over and see me tonight or if it's too late then tomorrow for sure. I'll be home all day."

Mariko nodded. Then it occurred to me to ask, "Did she ever mention a Mr. Slinger?"

Mariko looked shocked and shook her head vigorously, "No, no man!"

"Mariko, it's ok, I mean the man, Mr. Slinger, was her neighbour and I wondered if she was upset over his death. Did she ever say anything about him?"

"Oh, neighbor. No," she smiled, "No Slinger.   I would remember because of shoes."

I left her at the door and went back to the car puzzling over what she had said.   It's tricky talking with someone whose command of English is so shaky. I drove home and got the soup out of the trunk, hoping Minnie would show up later. As I climbed up my back stairs it hit me. I almost dropped the pot I was laughing so hard, Slinger, sling back shoes, of course.

CHAPTER 11

I put the soup back in the freezer thinking about what Mariko said. It didn't sound too terrible, just out of character for Minnie. And the fact that it had been going on for sometime made me uneasy. Mostly I felt guilty that I hadn't noticed anything before now. I mooched around, finally settling to watch a British murder mystery. It ended predictably, the handyman did it. Bob was the only handyman I knew with any connection to Slinger and he looked incapable of tying his own shoes.

It was still early when the doorbell rang. I jumped up hoping it was Minnie. I opened the door with a smile preparing to welcome her in. It was Jack.

We stared at each other for a moment then he cleared his throat, "Can I talk to you for a minute?"

"Sure," I was flustered, what was he doing here? I waved him to the living room.

He hung up his coat and settled himself in an armchair. The video cover was on the ottoman and he picked it up. "I like this one, the handyman did it."

"Yeah, I know. Good thing I finished watching it, I hate spoilers."

He looked at the TV screen, "Clever," he said as he pointed at the flat screen TV with my painting now slid to one side.

He sighed heavily then sat forward resting his arms on his thighs asking again, "Are you sure you didn't know Frank Slinger?"

Now I was annoyed. "I told you I didn't. Do you think I'm lying?"

"I don't really but," he spread his hands shrugging, "I had to ask. You live almost on the same block. It is reasonable."

"Good grief. I can assure you I never met the man."

"Okay, I just needed to make sure because of what I need to ask next. You see Frank Slinger was also a knitter."

"Really?" I was surprised, "I don't know any male knitters."

"Yeah, well he was one, or at least we are pretty sure he was." He paused, "Remember I asked you if you were an expert knitter."

I nodded.

"And beside that other lady who is in Paris, you indicated you were?"

"Yes, but you never told me the context and really that is the most important thing I need to know before I can say for sure."

He looked puzzled.

I tried to explain, "I'm not trying to avoid the question I just don't want to commit to something I don't understand. I mean," I took a deep breath trying to order my thoughts, "I can't imagine how my being an expert knitter or not could possibly help solve a crime."

"I know it's weird and frankly I have no idea if getting answers to some questions related to knitting will help." He ran his fingers down his chin. I recognized the mannerism, he did it when he was thinking. "Normally I don't have this problem.

An expert witness is an expert witness. They know the drill. I've never had to try to find an expert witness for something like knitting." He looked exasperated then seemed to make up his mind, "I have to ask that you not repeat anything I tell you, at least not at this point. We are trying to keep this quiet. So even if you don't think you can help us you still can't mention anything. Agreed?"

I was intrigued, "Okay."

"It's a bit macabre but a knitting needle was the murder weapon," he said, watching me closely.

I sat back with a thud. "Yuck!"

He continued, "Somehow the press got hold of that bit of information so it will be on the news tomorrow. Though the rest of what I tell you needs to be kept confidential."

The shock was wearing off. I nodded, curious, "So that was the real reason why you thought I might know Slinger. Because of knitting?"

"Yes, and remember that was before we talked to your neighbor."

"I hope this doesn't make me give up knitting," I smiled faintly. "How exactly was it used?"

"He was stabbed through the throat. Right here." And he pointed to the little hollow in his neck.

"What a horrible way to die! Was it fast?"

"The coroner says yes, that he probably had no idea. There wasn't even a look of surprise on his face."

We sat in silence.

Finally he pulled an envelope out of his jacket pocket. "Do you think you could have a look at some photos of the crime scene and tell me anything that might strike you?"

Suddenly I was squeamish. It was one thing to speculate about a murder it was another to see it. "Was there much blood? I mean I can handle blood but not if it's really gruesome." I said sheepishly.

"I think you'll find these bearable. I only brought a few that highlight the knitting angle and only in black and white so it's not too graphic."

"Okay I'll give it a try." I didn't say aloud the reservations I still felt. And what difference was a knitting needle to say a kitchen knife or BBQ fork as a murder weapon? He was the detective he should be able to figure that out, there must be more to it if he needed my help.

He seemed to know what I was thinking. He held onto the photos. "The fact that a needle was used to stab Slinger may be of no significance, it could just be that it was handy and so not pre-meditated. But I have to cover all the possibilities and as no one on the force knows anything about knitting if you can just have a look I'd really appreciate it."

He was holding his head to one side like Rocco the german shepherd, I melted on the spot and nodded, "Fine, show me."

He spread the photos on the ottoman. 5 shots, 5 angles. One showed Slinger with the needle the other four were of the area around the chair in which he was sitting. They weren't terrible at all and as Jack said the fact that they were in black and white helped.

I picked up one that showed the corner of the chair and one of Slinger's slipper clad feet. Terrible slippers, I stifled a nervous giggle.

"What?" Jack asked expectantly.

"Nothing." I replied blushing.

"Nothing is nothing. Tell me. You never know, it could be important," he said seriously.

"Well, this is nothing," I said as he glared at me, "I just think he has terrible slippers!"

"Oh." He let out a deep sigh.

Somehow the exchange helped relax me. I looked at the next photo turning it upside down. It was a knitting pattern. I couldn't actually read much, the paper was creased and the photo wasn't taken to highlight the printing though I could read the title, Picot Edged Diamond Dishcloth.

"Was Slinger knitting this?"

"Keep going." He was content to wait.

I picked up the next. It again showed the chair with a cloth bag leaning against it. I could see more yarn, needles and papers in the bag. I looked up, but he just nodded to the photos.

Shaking my head, I studied an image that I realized with a start was Slinger's lap. His hands were resting comfortably on the arms of the chair and on his lap was, I guessed, an almost completed picot edged diamond dishcloth. There was only one knitting needle. I put the photo down and went back to the first one, looking at the strand of yarn dangling to the floor ending in a bundle of yarn. Frowning, I looked at the last. Slinger sat upright in his chair. He looked comfortable, like he was settled in for a night of TV and knitting. There was no surprise on his face, just as Jack said. In fact he looked content, almost smug. If you ignored the fact that there was a needle sticking out of his neck he looked like he might invite me to join him in a stitch 'n bitch session.

Jack broke into my thoughts, "So is there anything that strikes you as interesting?"

"Well, it's obvious that Slinger is the knitter," I began. "He looks so comfortable and the bag, its full of the stuff a knitter needs. And if it wasn't his then you would be that much closer to the killer, I presume"

"Yes, we agree he's the knitter."

"What I don't understand is everything else." I pointed to the photo of his lap. "There is only one needle in his lap and the one in his throat isn't the same. It looks like the one in his neck is metal and the one on his lap plastic. Is that right?"

"Yes, we thought maybe he was just knitting with odd needles, we've been told they are the same size."

"I suppose so. Frankly I have never heard of a knitter choosing to use the same size but two different needles on a project. I mean some patterns require that you use 2 different sizes of needle to create a specific effect. But something as simple as a dishcloth? Are you sure they are the same size?"

He nodded, "Forensics checked."

"So that is really strange. Knitters usually have preference for a particular type of needle; metal, plastic, bamboo or whatever. I suppose there are knitters who don't care and will use any needle that comes to hand," I shook my head. "Still it's odd. And if it is deliberate, it really doesn't make any sense. I'll have to think about it."

"That is all very interesting from a knitting point of view but I'm not sure it helps me."

"Sorry, I don't know what it means yet, you just asked me what I could tell you about the knitting."

"I'm sorry too," he apologized. "This case is just so frustrating. Basically what we have is a dead man, killed with his own knitting needle as he sat in his chair. The needles didn't give up any fingerprints. There isn't anything but a few smudges so whoever killed him either wore gloves, which seems unlikely given that Slinger let him in, sat down, took up his knitting and the killer still hadn't taken off his gloves or the killer wiped the needle while it was still in his throat."

"That doesn't sound easy." Jack nodded in agreement. "Maybe he said his hands were cold and kept his gloves on," I offered.

"Right. So the murderer came in, stabbed him and left. That's what we've come up with too. We still haven't found any other forensics to directly connect a killer to Slinger even though we found tons of different sets of fingerprints, shoe prints and fibres all from different people. You'd have guessed that Slinger held a big house party the day he died."

We sat in silence. "Oh well, it was a long shot," he said. "Don't worry about it." He bent to gather the photos.

I waved him off saying, "There are two more things that don't make sense."

I stared at the photos. "Was he right or left handed?" I asked. That got his attention.

"Right, why?"

"Then the knitting is backwards. " I pointed to the photo of his lap, "it might not mean anything but it's odd."

"What do you mean?"

I looked around, there was a magazine so I picked it up and opened it at random. "Okay so I'm reading this and I put it on my lap because someone comes in. Right?"

"Yeah"

"But the knitting on his lap is like this" and I twisted the magazine around.

"You think it was done by the killer?"

I nodded, "I suppose there are reasons a killer would do that. For instance, get it out of the way to do something else or move it to cover something."

Jack nodded in agreement. "You said two things, what's the second?"

"The wool on the floor. Is this exactly how you found it?"

"Yes"

"I can't really tell. It just looks wrong, almost like it was placed or messed up on purpose or something. Do you have any more photos of this, better shots, maybe in color? And maybe I could see the actual dishcloth and ball of yarn?"

"I don't have anything on me but I can bring by more photos. I'll have to get you identified as an expert witness before I could show them to you. Would that be okay? "

"It's your call. At this point I can't tell you anything more without more information but I am willing to help." I paused a moment before adding, "So if you could get a copy of the pattern and a list of what exactly was in his knitting bag and a sample of the yarn he was using or at least the name?"

He grinned, "You're sounding more like an expert witness by the second!"

"Don't expect too much. I still don't see how answering these questions will help you find your killer. Though I admit that I am intrigued."

"That's good enough for me. Even if it has no bearing on the actual murder we still need to answer any questions that might be raised and frankly the knitting angle is a new one. Let's see," he paused, "it'll take me a bit to get you on record as an expert and then get your information.   How about Tuesday morning?"

I nodded, agreeing to meet at a local coffee shop.

CHAPTER 12

It wasn't a date but that's what Jen called it when I ran into her the following morning and told her about my meeting with Jack.

She and I go to the same gym. On Monday mornings I like the early hot yoga class and I came out pulling a huge sweatshirt over my sweaty self. I was rushing for the door knowing that if I was fast I could get home and into a shower before I got too chilled.

Jen was coming out of a spin class. I gazed at her in wonder. Not a hair was out of place; she was in pale lavender, a matching Lululemon set. My sweatshirt was one I used for painting till it got too ratty. She was glowing. Sweat was dripping into my eyes and my bare thighs were an odd shade of puce, radiating heat.

We walked quickly to our cars. "You set a time and a place to meet, that makes it a date," Jen said firmly.

"Yeah well I do the same thing when I want my hair cut or an oil change! Anyway," I grinned, "how would you know a real date from a play date, Miss Married with Children?"

She smiled, her eyebrows raised, "Play dates involve little people, this involves a real man," she said smugly.

She was right, "Okay, it's business date," I conceded.

"What are you going to wear?" she asked as she unlocked her car.

"Wear? You sound like Tessa! Why is everyone so interested in what I wear?"

"You haven't been so interested in a man before."

"What's that got to do with what I wear, what I have always worn." I stopped and raised my hand, "Never mind don't answer that." I protested, "And I'm not interested."

"Amy, really, are you kidding me?"

"I don't even know if he is married or has 6 toes or anything!"

"Well, you're not going to find out if you scare him away wearing sweats are you?"

"That's not fair, I'm wearing sweats because I just came from yoga."

"I know," she smiled, "anyway, that was a good idea."

"What Idea?" I sometimes feel that talking with Jen is like being on a playground, she jumps from topic to topic like kids on a trampoline.

"To ask Tessa what you should wear," she replied as patiently as she would to her 6 year old and drove off.

I got into my car. Tessa and Jen were right, this wasn't about Jack. He really had nothing to do with it, I needed this for me. Jack was just a speed bump that reminded me to pay attention. I was in a rut. It was just a matter of time before things really got out of hand and I stopped brushing my hair or teeth every day. So while meeting Jack might be the motivator I wasn't really doing it for him. In any case it was too late for me to try to impress him with the new me. Face it; he'd seen me at my worse. No, I admitted, if he saw me now that would be my worse.

As I parked in front of my house I looked around frantically. Jack had a disturbing tendency to show up when I looked like

I was masquerading as a garbage dump. I ran and made it into the house without a sighting. Throwing the sweatshirt in the garbage as I passed I headed for the shower. As I rubbed shampoo into my hair I made a mental list. First, I needed to talk to Minnie. I was concerned about how glum she'd been at the service and wondering why she ran off so suddenly. How well did she know Slinger? Mariko's reaction to a mention of a man in Minnie's life stunned me. Was Minnie closer to Slinger than I imagined. She had to know him well enough to know he was a bully. Could they have been in a relationship? I didn't think it was likely, I knew her too well. We spent too much time together for her not to ever let slip that there was a man, of any description, in her life. But was that really the case? I realized I'd seen less of her over the last few months. Did that have anything to do with the murder? The sting of shampoo in my eyes roused me. It was imperative I talk to Minnie.

I got out of the shower, dressed and called her. Still no answer, but Mariko must have given her my message. I made up my mind, if I didn't hear from her by noon I was going to go over there and not leave till I found out what was going on.

I called Tessa and got voice mail. Rather than watch the clock I started work on a basset hound for June. I was lost in Ben's sad eyes when the doorbell rang.

With my brush in hand I went to the door. Minnie looked more frail than I ever imagined she could.

I opened the door wider, "Oh Minnie, come in."

"You're painting. I'll come back later," she said and turned away.

"Oh no you don't!" I smiled catching her by the arm, "I need a break. How about a nice cup of tea?"

Minnie smiled wanly. I helped her in the door, hung up her coat and settled her in a chair in the kitchen. I went into my studio plunging the brush in water and taking a piece of plastic wrap to quickly cover my palette.

Minnie was sitting where I left her, her purse clutched in her hands.

Smiling brightly I said, "I need a cup of tea. How about you? English Breakfast or fennel?"

Minnie was looking out the window into the garden. Fennel, I decided. It looked like she wasn't eating properly and fennel would be better on an empty stomach.

We didn't talk as I sliced some apple bread I'd made and added a few slices of cheddar to a plate.

When the tea was ready I sat down opposite, poured her a cup and when she didn't seem to notice, took her hand gently and wrapped it around the cup.

She looked up gratefully and took a tiny sip. I watched as she visibly relaxed.

"Here, it's that apple bread you like and a nice strong cheddar." I pushed the plate closer to her.

She looked like she might refuse and then changed her mind. After another cup of tea and a few more mouthfuls, the grey defeated look slipped away though she still looked dreadfully tired.

"What's going on Minnie? Mariko is very concerned and I'm worried too. I saw you at the service for Slinger and then you just ran off."

She sat staring at her cup.

"Minnie, I really want to help."

Finally she looked up and then began to cry, tiny droplets that collected in the corners of her eyes, "Amy, I just don't know what to do."

I reached across the table and gave her hand a squeeze then got up and grabbed a box of tissues, handing her one. "Tell me."

She placed her teacup gently in its saucer saying wearily, "It's a long story."

I smiled, "I've got lots of time."

She took a deep breath, "You never knew my husband, Arthur. He was a good man, a good husband in many ways. After he died I realized that money management wasn't something he did well. He took care of our finances and I found out we had very little money." She paused. "Anyway I had to teach myself pretty fast so I sat down with all my bills and worked out exactly how much money I needed every month. It was discouraging. Between my pension and our savings I knew I could only last a couple of years before I would have to sell the house and I didn't want to do that."

"Minnie, I knew things were tight but I had no idea. You could have come to me."

"How could I? I'd just met you and you were just beginning to make a living at painting. Actually you were probably in about the same situation as me; just half my age," she said somewhat shrewdly, I thought.

She continued, "I decided I needed income. I haven't worked for 30 years so trying to get my old job was out of the question. I thought of a bed and breakfast. I got some books out of the library about setting up a business and realized the income isn't steady and when it is you have do so much laundry. I hate laundry," she said with a weak smile. "Then I thought of getting in students, English language or exchange students. So I contacted a service and got my first student. The kids are great company. Sometimes they help around the house and the money they bring in helps."

I nodded adding, "I admire you for the care you take of your students. I'm sure that you give them more in terms of motherly care than they give you in money."

"Thank you Amy, you are kind. It's true I sometimes mother them, they are so alone and in a foreign country. I do my best."

"So what went wrong?"

She took a deep breath, her voice shaking, "Did you ever meet Ken? He was here last fall. The last student I had before Mariko."

I shook my head.

"Ken was from Korea. From the very first he was different. He never seemed to go to school even though he was here as a student. And the first thing he wanted when he arrived was high speed internet with maximum data. I didn't even know what that was but he was willing to pay for it so I agreed. Later I checked with the student placement people and they assured me that his request wasn't unusual. They explained that most foreign students are lonely and spend a lot of time either talking to their friends at home or playing games on their computers and that takes data."

"For the first few weeks it was fine, I mean he seemed to stay up all night and sleep during the day but I wasn't meant to monitor his school attendance so I left him alone. He was also easy to feed. As long as I had rice, eggs and instant pot noodle soups he was happy. I tried making dishes he might like but he was always very polite, said no and boiled water for another bowl of noodles. He did discover hot dogs and after that ate a lot of them as well."

"He doesn't sound too much different from other foreign students I've heard about." I said.

"I guess not but he was different from my other students. It was later that things went wrong." She looked like she might start crying again and was obviously embarrassed.

"We need more tea! Just relax for a minute while I make some more. Or would you rather have some soup? I have a pot in the freezer."

Minnie shook her head.

I stood at the counter waiting for the kettle to boil and thought about what Minnie had said so far and what it meant.

CHAPTER 13

When we were both fortified by more tea, I prompted her to continue her story, "Minnie, it can't be that bad."

"Oh yes it can!" she said with a bit of her old spunk. I was glad to see that she was relaxing enough to make a small joke.

She took a deep breath and continued, "One of the rules I insist on with all my students is that they are not allowed in my bedroom and I don't enter their's. I feel we each need our own space."

"Sounds like a good rule."

"I think so. I have a small cabinet outside their bedroom door. It's a place for me to leave things for them. Clean sheets, towels, mail, snacks, that sort of thing. Normally I do laundry the same day every week and the students know it, they strip their beds and leave the dirty sheets on the cabinet, I wash them and return them later in the day."

I remembered Mariko mentioning that routine.

"But that week a repairman was coming to fix a leak and he'd already said that he would have to turn off the water to the washer for a couple of days while he replaced the piping. I told Ken of the change in laundry day but he left in the morning and forgot to leave his sheets out. So I broke my own rule."

She looked sad and guilty saying, "I wish I never had!" Then continued more calmly, "Too late now. Anyway I thought I'd just pop in, strip the bed and tell him when he got back. I went in and pulled off the bedspread, that's when I saw them, on a shelf under the desk."

"What?"

Wringing her hands she looked mystified, "Cell phones. At least three dozen cell phones. They were all different kinds and looked new. A few of them were plugged in and the rest were laying on the shelf."

"Cell phones, what could anyone want with that many?"

"I don't know! All I know is that he was hiding them."

"On a shelf in his room? To be fair, they weren't really hidden."

Minnie shook her head, "But my rule means that I never enter his room and from the door you couldn't see them. I only found them because I came right into the room."

"Right. So what did you do?"

"I put the bedspread back on and left."

"Did he say anything?"

"No, I don't think he even knew I'd been in but from then on I didn't like him. I didn't trust him, you see."

"Of course you didn't. What happened next?"

"I didn't know what to do. I mean, he might have a reasonable explanation. A few days later he announced that he was leaving early. I was so relieved, I just didn't want to cause any trouble."

"So what's the problem?"

Minnie sniffed back her tears, "A couple of days before he was due to go I got a visit from Frank Slinger."

"Slinger!"

"Yes. He said that Ken was using my house for illegal deals and since Ken was under my care, I was an accessory."

"What kind of deals?"

"He said drugs but I don't know. He said he'd tell the authorities and I wouldn't get any more students. Besides the money they bring in, I like having a student with me, until that last month with Ken I feel safer with someone else in the house." Her eyes pleaded with me to understand, "So I didn't say anything and Ken went home."

"What did Slinger do?"

"The day after Ken left I got another visit. This time he said that even though Ken was gone the problem hadn't. He still threatened to call the placement service, all of them. I'd never be able to have another student. Then he said he heard I was a good cook and if I supplied two dinners a week he would keep his mouth closed."

"He blackmailed you for frozen dinners?" I was incredulous.

She nodded miserably, "It wasn't really blackmail, was it? I mean I often give meals to neighbors."

"Maybe, but not two every week. It may be ridiculous but it's still blackmail. He never asked for money or anything else?"

Minnie was appalled. "No never! Even so it was awful. He was so demanding about the food, didn't like this or that."

I ignored his dinner preferences, "How much of this does Mariko know?"

"Nothing," Minnie smiled briefly, "she is such a sweet girl."

"Well, she knows you've been unhappy, she told me. You better let her know that you're not mad at her. She seems quite upset."

"Oh dear, I had no idea," Minnie was distressed.

"Just talk to her, you don't need to tell her the whole story but you will have to give her a reason for the missing lasagna, " I smiled, "she noticed that!"

Minnie seemed to relax. Telling me the story seemed to take a load off her shoulders.
"What should I do," she asked?

"In all honesty, Minnie, I don't think you need to worry anymore. Slinger is dead and that's the end of the story."

"But what about the dinners that are still in his freezer. My fingerprints will be all over them. They'll wonder why I was giving him frozen dinners."

"Minnie, I am sure that the police are not interested in the contents of Slingers freezer. In any case if they ask just tell them you often give food to neighbors. As you've said, it's the truth. I'll even back you up, you've brought me some wonderful casseroles." I smiled adding, "But if you want, I can talk to Inspector Sommerville about it."

Minnie panicked, "Oh no, don't do that!"

I patted her hand, "You can't keep worrying about it. The real problem is that Slinger may have taken advantage of other people as well and one of them may be the killer. Perhaps his blackmailing took in far more serious things than frozen dinners."

WAS

"I know, I getting up the courage to tell the police when I heard about the needle.   Who else knits?" Minnie asked quietly.

I realized she was right. If Minnie told the police her story she would be a prime suspect. I thought rapidly, "If we don't tell them about Ken and Slinger they may find out anyway and that may be worse for you. Somehow we need to point them in the direction of any other blackmail victims so that when they find out about you it won't be so bad.   I'm positive blackmail is a lead they haven't pursued."   I made up my mind, "Do you have any idea who else he could have blackmailed?"

Minnie shook her head.

"What about the people at the service?   The Richters, Bob from the church and that snoopy next door neighbour. Maybe even the Reverend Harper."   I might be clutching at straws but right now anyone was a better target for the police to pursue than Minnie.

GRASPING

"Really I have no idea," Minnie said forlornly.

Thinking of the service I asked, "By the way, why did you run off after the memorial? In fact why did you even go in the first place?"

"I don't know, I just wanted to make sure he was dead I guess but then I saw that policeman and I got frightened."

Frightened of Jack?   Hard to believe but then he did have a way of getting more information than giving it. I wondered if she was holding something back.   "You have told me everything haven't you?"   Minnie stared at her hands and nodded. I waited but she didn't say anything or look up. There was something still bothering her. I tried a different tack, "On knit night when we heard the police were going from door to door you said 'how'. What did you mean?"

Minnie answered quickly, "Did I say that?"

I nodded.

She said hesitantly, as though she was making it up as she went along, "I was wondering how they found out about me so fast?"

It sounded like a half-truth but I let it go. Another question occurred to me, "How do you think Slinger found out about Ken?"

"I don't know for sure but Slinger was a snoop. I once found him on my front step putting down a parcel. It was for Ken. Slinger said it was delivered to the wrong address. Now I know he was retired from the post office by then, so what was he doing with it?"

I thought for a bit, "He could have opened it and figured out what Ken was up to. Maybe Slinger was blackmailing Ken as well."

"Do you think so?"

"Why not? It would explain why Ken left early. And I think the murder must be about blackmail, you can't be his only victim."

Minnie was finally starting the thaw. She no longer looked frightened and old, she was regaining her confidence and said, "Just telling you makes me feel so much better." She smiled. "I'll go home right now and make a lasagna for Mariko."

"Good idea," I said as she put on her coat. "One more thing, what happened to Ken? Have you heard from him at all?"

"No, but the school called to say he was coming back for another semester and asked if I wanted to have him stay with me."

"And you told them no"

She smiled, "I told them I didn't like his late nights."

"I'd still like to know what's he up to. And eventually if we find out anything about Ken I think we will have to tell the school or the police. What's his full name and the name of the school?"

She gave me the information adding "You won't say anything about me, will you?

"No, For now I'll just inquire about taking in a student myself."

After she left, I smiled; the case of the missing lasagna was solved! Then I frowned; the problem was that the answer to that riddle opened up a whole new set of questions about the murder. Did the police know about the blackmail? Did they know about Ken? Was whatever he was doing unlawful? Should I tell Jack? I promised not to tell the police about Minnie but didn't say anything about Ken. How could I tell Jack about Ken without involving Minnie? It was impossible. I would just have to find out more before I said anything. It was even possible the police already knew about the blackmail angle.

I rinsed the cups, thinking about Minnie and blackmail. The only way to keep her from coming under scrutiny was to try to find a different blackmail victim and I knew just where to start.

The Reverend Harper said to call on her, so I would. I was curious why she wanted to talk to me and she knew the people I thought might be victims. She could be the key.

While I dialled ~~dialled~~ *dialed* I wondered if a woman could have the physical strength to commit the murder? It looked easy. Just stick it in, like skewering a piece of meat for the barbecue. Physically it looked possible for a man or woman to do it but when it was a human neck? I cringed. It was insane but could Minnie have done it? Did she have the strength? It was preposterous or was it?

Reverend Harper picked up on the third ring. She didn't sound surprised to hear from me. She wasn't available until the next evening and then only between an AA meeting and a Boy Scout gathering, we set a time to meet at the church.

Seconds later Tessa called, "Ready for a little retail therapy?"

I really had no excuse. There wasn't anything I could do about Minnie's problem until my meeting with the Reverend and I was caught up on my work so I let Tessa talk me into a shopping session.

"Cheer up, it will be an adventure," she said.

"Like a root canal," I grimaced. "You know I really hate the whole process of shopping."

"Amy, I promise it'll be fun. Trust me."

"I don't want to have fun I just want to come home to a closet magically full of fabulous goodies and fewer sweats. By the way I have two rules about shopping, I need lots of stress breaks preferably with an iced coffee."

"Done. And the second?" Tessa asked suspiciously.

"No change rooms. I don't do change rooms. They are too small with trick mirrors and they smell." I explained.

"Trick mirrors?"

"Everything looks fine in the store but when I get home I'm still dumpy, frumpy, lumpy and now grumpy," I said crossly.

"I admit they are not my favourite places."

"I'll give you one chance to fix me," I teased only half serious. "After that I'm joining a nudist colony."

Tessa laughed and said she would be right over, "I have to get out of the house anyway, Rose is here and she doesn't like me to be in the house when she cleans."

"Did you ask her about Slinger?"

She lowered her voice, "Yes, all she said was that he was bad and when I mentioned that he drove for charity she got very red in the face and said and I quote, "Yeah for the free gas. He also said he knit for the homeless. I bet he wanted the free soup! He did nothing for anyone."

"It sounds like she knew him well enough to dislike him."

"Yes. We can talk about it later. You know elephants!" she laughed and hung up.

CHAPTER 14

Elephants? "What was that about elephants?" I asked as soon as she came to my door.

"Big ears, you know. Rose came into the room."

I laughed. "Do you think Rose knew Slinger well enough to be a suspect for his murder?"

Tessa was startled, "Are you serious?" When she saw that I was she took a moment to answer, "No, I don't know her well enough. I only ever see her occasionally, she really doesn't like it if I'm home when she cleans and that's fine by me. I guess it was a bit strange to see her at the memorial service though," she mused.

"WHAT! You never told me she was there."

"Didn't you see her?"

"I've never met her, I have no idea what she looks like!"

"Oh, sorry, " Tessa said patiently, "she was the one in army boots."

I remembered the woman and her look of fury. "Have the police talked with her? Does Jack know who she is and that she must know Slinger?"

"I don't know. You'll have to ask him."

I planned to. Meanwhile we were supposed to be going shopping. I picked up my keys, "Your car or mine," I asked?

"Whoa, we're not going anywhere yet. First we need to see what you have. We need to know what we have to work with."

"You mean we're not going now?" I was grateful and disappointed at the same time. I was all geared up and Tessa was putting the breaks on. "I need something new to wear tomorrow."

"For what?" she asked.

"An appointment" I said shortly. There was no way I was telling her about my meeting with Jack. I decided to change the subject, "How was your date with Jeff?"

"Interesting."

"Is that it? Is that all you are going to tell me?"

Tessa smiled.

"Fine, then I'll put on the kettle."

"Okay and I'll tackle the closet."

My bedroom closet is very small, a standard size cupboard with one rod plus under-the-bed bins for sweaters, purses, belts and scarves.

By the time I came in with the tea my closet was bare and the bed was covered with clothes. I looked at it in despair, "I might as well take the whole mess to the Sally Ann."

"That's not true, you need a good overhaul but you do have some nice pieces. What you have on is good, add this down vest and you can wear it on your date."

"It's NOT a date!" I grimaced, how did she guess I was meeting Jack? Jen must have told her. "Knitters are terrible gossips," I said pointedly.

"Okay, okay, your appointment. Keep your shirt on. Let's get to work. We need to go through his pile and sort it into keep, fix, donate, and trash."

We started with the slacks. As predicted I would rather have my teeth pulled. After more than an hour Tessa announced, "that was a good start. "

Actually, I was surprised that there were more things in the keep and fix pile than I guessed possible. After we bundled up the other two piles she spread out the remaining clothes and took photos with my phone. She spent a lot of time, explaining the need to get the photo as close to the real thing as possible to use it to color match when shopping.

I was impressed, "What a good idea."

"I know," she said smugly, "anyway, if you hate shopping I guarantee that you hate returning even more."

"Exactly!"

"That's enough for one day, let's put up our feet, order a pizza, have a glass of wine and watch a Dr. Who, the one with the dishy Doctor."

"Great idea! I'm loving your idea of shopping."

The next morning I tentatively opened my eyes, not quite a headache though not all that brisk either. The empty bottle of wine stared at me from the kitchen counter. I went to the basement to get a jar of peaches for a smoothie.

There was no sign of Tom Smooch, he wasn't in the laundry basket but a dirty towel was. I looked at the smear, knowing I'd have to get it soaking but didn't feel up to the effort and headed back upstairs.

I wasn't too worried about Tom Smooch. He was only an infrequent visitor. Now that Slinger wasn't around, were other neighbors looking after him? If he drifted around the neighborhood from meal to meal that would explain his weight. I decided to ask Jack about him.

Showering helped clear my head and when I put on the outfit Tessa set out the day before I felt even better. I decided to skip coffee and made my smoothie. Heading to my studio, I made a start on two ferrets for July. I named them Fred and Ginger and their tumbling fight became a grand tango, we all had a good time.

When it was finally time to go it was raining so I decided to drive even though the coffee shop is an easy walk from my house. Jack was already there reading through a file. He stood when he saw me and started to come up to the front. I waved him back to his seat and placed my order, quad espresso over ice. That would kick my mini-hangover on its heels or it would kill me. Either way I die happy.

Jack raised his eyebrows when he saw my drink. "Hair of the dog?"

"How did you know?" I laughed.

It was warm and snug in the coffee shop. It was roasting day and the aroma was intoxicating. A fire was burning and the armchair was inviting. I sat back taking a deep gulp.

The caffeine kicked in and I felt better. "What a lovely day!" I said exuberantly.

He looked at me, his grey eyes stormy, "It's raining, I dropped my coat in a puddle as I was getting in my car. My sergeant is off sick and I haven't solved this case," he said then smiled, "although I have to admit it's getting better."

"Oh," I was suddenly self-conscious.

He leaned forward and set the file he was reading on the coffee table. He was good at that, saying something nice and then becoming all business. A one man good cop/bad cop. It was unsettling. How did criminals feel under this technique? Or his wife or girlfriend? I took a deep gulp, more caffeine, that's what I needed to feel ready when he began.

"First, I have convinced my super that you are our expert witness. That really doesn't mean anything now but if we do need testimony in court you'll have to be the one. On the other hand if the knitting angle has nothing to do with the solution to the crime you will just be the consultant on file."

I nodded my agreement.

"Good, because otherwise I can't show you the photos." He dug in his briefcase and pulled out another file. He flipped through some pages, "Here they are. Just remember everything is confidential. Have a look through them; take all the time you need. Some of them aren't very pleasant but I think you'll find that they aren't too gruesome."

There must have been two dozen shots in the pile. The first few were the ones I'd already seen in black and white so I put them aside and flipped quickly through the rest, I didn't want any nasty surprises when I looked through them properly. When I got to the end I was relieved to find them manageable.

In color the scenes looked totally different, more vivid, more graphic, and more distressing. I tried not to flinch as I went through the pile more slowly. They were well lit, with careful attention to detail, clinical. The photos were all in a jumble; kitchen, living room, chair, head shot, knitting bag. I looked around, there was only one other person in the coffee shop and we had the fireplace corner to ourselves. "Can I fan these out?" I asked. Jack nodded. I laid the head shot in the middle of the table and started placing each of the other photos how they were connected, working like each was part of a jigsaw. I put the full body photo of Slinger partially under the headshot. The knitting bag went on the left and a little lower down, the kitchen over his right shoulder, the ball of yarn on the floor in front of him. I kept placing the photos; overlapping and leaving gaps until they were in place. It made a rough finished puzzle.

"Can I take a photo of this?" I asked.

He seemed intrigued, "I don't see why not, as long as you keep it to yourself," he answered and took the same shot with his phone.

I sat back studying the scene and sipping my iced coffee. "Did you bring the other things I asked for?"

He dug two sheets of paper out of the file; pattern, yarn type and knitting bag list.

I studied the lists, "Okay here's what I can tell at first glance."

Jack got out a pen and notebook, "Go ahead."

I picked my words carefully conscious that I was speaking as an expert witness. "So the two different needles make no sense. He is knitting with one plastic and one metal needle. No one does that when they have the other needle in the pair."

"What do you mean?"

"Well, when I first saw the two different needles I thought maybe he liked knitting with plastic needles and that he lost or broke one and so was making do till he could get a new pair."

"Yeah, so?"

"Now I see he has the mate to each set in his bag. See, it's on the list," I pointed to one of the papers. "By the way whoever made this list doesn't know the first thing about knitting," I said.

"I know. That is why we called in the expert," he grinned.

"It doesn't take an expert to realize that knitting needles come in pairs so why each needle is listed separately is just weird."

"I'll tell Constable Bradley you said that."

"That makes perfect sense. Constable Bradley! I wouldn't trust him with my grocery list. You realize he licks his pencil and there is a connection between lead poisoning and brain damage!" I laughed.

Jack looked like he might agree but diplomatically changed the subject, "Anyway, two different needles, what does that tell you?"

"It's interesting, I'll have to think about it," I said truthfully and put the paper down. I picked up the photo of the pile of yarn at his feet, "Is that blood on the yarn?"

"Yes."

I looked at it grimly. "Is this normal? I mean from a puncture wound in the throat to see so little blood and why on the floor in front of him?"

"Apparently from the angle of the wound he was leaning slightly forward when he was stabbed. And because of the angle it didn't bleed much and so only a little dripped in front of him and onto the wool."

"But the blood stain doesn't seem to be on top of the pile of wool."

"I wondered if you would notice that. We think he was leaning forward, stabbed and the blood dripped. Then the killer kicked the pile or Slinger caught it with his foot as he was stabbed and fell back into the chair."

"Don't you think that if someone kicked it then it would be more disarranged? I mean, it's a very neat pile."

"Can you think of another explanation?"

"There are actually three problems, the neatness, the unravelling and the blood placement. "

He nodded encouragingly.

"Its like this. When you knit, the yarn comes off the ball smoothly, see that bit at the bottom. Now look at the yarn on top, see how it is all squiggly? That's what happens when you unravel knitting. It's called frogging when you make a mistake and have to go backwards and re-knit. If I had to guess I would say that Slinger was unraveling his project when the killer struck. That explains the squiggly yarn at the top though it doesn't make sense that the blood is underneath or why the pile as a whole is so neat. I mean, for the blood to be on the bottom he had to be stabbed, drip, then unravel." I sat back, "Is it even possible?"

"You mean how long he did it take him to die and could he function enough to knit?"

I nodded.

"I'd have to ask the pathologist. But as I said before frankly I don't think so."

"If Slinger didn't do it then the only other explanation I can think of," I looked at Jack and said slowly, "is that someone else, like the killer, did the frogging." I didn't mention that only a knitter would be able to do that, a knitter like Minnie.

There was a long pause, "Anything else?" he asked.

"Can you tell me anything else about the investigation?"

"Like what?"

"Like who identified the body? Who is the next of kin? Who doesn't have an alibi?"

"Why do you want to know?"

I avoided the question, "I am an expert witness, why shouldn't I know?"

"We are still checking."

I raised my eyebrows in disbelief.

"It's early days, but we'll get there." Jack glanced at his watch. "I'm sorry, I have to get going. You brought up some interesting questions. I'll see if I can get you some answers. Meanwhile, give me a call if anything occurs to you or you need anything else."

"Um, can I have a look at the whole file?"

"Sorry, it's confidential."

"Your expert witness can't see it?"

He paused, looking around, "Can you just watch my things," he nodded to the files, "I'll be right back," and he headed off to the washroom.

Smooth, he was very smooth. I ignored the file with the photos and picked up the other one, leafing through it quickly. Flipping through the reports of interrogations with neighbors Minnie's name jumped out. An Officer, not Bradley I was happy to see, interviewed her. He called her elderly and frail. From my point of view that was good news. The bad news was that there wasn't much information on anyone else. Frowning, I guessed that somewhere there was a more comprehensive file. This wasn't it so I laid it back on the table. I smiled innocently when Jack came back.

"Get everything you need?" He asked.

"Yes, thank you. I did have a couple of additional questions. There was an angry lady at the service in a brown coat, Tessa said it was her cleaning lady, Rose Tomson, do you know what she was doing there?"

"Not really, Reverend Harper said she cleaned for the church. Why? Do you think she's important?"

"Well, Rose told Tessa that Slinger was awful."

"She probably knew him from the church."

"Perhaps. But it sounds like Slinger didn't have many friends. What if Rose knew him well enough to be an enemy?"

He raised his eyebrows, "That's stretching it. Next?"

"What about the rest of the people from the memorial? You did say that anyone who attended might be a suspect."

"Like you, Tessa and Minnie?"

I tried to hide my chagrin, "Obviously not us!"

"Yeah, well, Carl Reid, the next door neighbor, and Fred Birch, the postie, don't have good alibis. The only one with a rock solid one is the Reverend."

"Any of them looking good as suspects?"

He looked at me so intently I blushed. Then he said blandly, "Anything else?"

"I wanted to ask about Tom"

Jack looked puzzled.

"Tom Smooch"

"Oh yeah," he grinned, "what about him?"

"Do you know if someone is looking after him?"

"All I know is that he's not been around Slinger's house. If he starts hanging around we'll have to call animal control."

"Please don't do that! If you see him call me, I'll look after him temporarily."

"Okay. Remember to call if anything occurs to you, anything at all. And I'll let you know about the other info."

I had no idea what I was getting into and I wasn't thinking about Tom Smooch.

CHAPTER 15

Even after I got home I couldn't stop thinking about the murder. The Case of the Missing Lasagna or The Knitting Needle Murder, innocent titles for a Ms. Marple mystery. But this wasn't fiction, this was real, a man was dead and however peculiar the circumstances it wasn't a joke. Jane Marple always said there were no real coincidences, that everything was connected. Was Port Oxford becoming St. Mary Mead?

I remembered to call the English language school and had almost been talked into interviewing for a student myself before I got the information I was seeking. Ken Kim, Minnie's ex-student was due back "any day now" to begin another session of school. Another dead end. He couldn't have murdered Slinger, he wasn't even here, though he could still be a blackmail victim. Contacting him would be a last resort. Until I knew the whole story about the cell phones he scared me. I was vague about my plans and told the secretary I'd be in touch. Even if I found out nothing more, I felt the school deserved to hear at least what Minnie knew.

My next step was my meeting with Jane later tonight so I spent the rest of the day immersed in my painting. After dinner, I headed to the church. I was early and found the Reverend standing in the aisle staring at the altar. Was she praying? Hating to   disturb her I whispered, "Reverend Harper."

"Oh. Sorry, wool gathering!" She laughed, "There's no need to whisper, welcome to our home," she waved her arm in the open space.

I smiled at the warm welcome. Looking around, I couldn't see anyone.

"Mine and the Big Guy," she said with a grin, "we share."

Today she was open and relaxed, not at all troubled and not at all like a blackmail victim. My time was short, I got straight to the point, "I'm wondering why you wanted to talk with me."

She looked at me, picking her words carefully, "You asked about Frank Slinger and I thought that if you took me up on my offer and came in for a chat then you might be the right person to chat with about him. This isn't something I would share with the police. I've heard that he was nosey."

I laid my cards on the table, "Honestly, as I said, I didn't know the man. I think, from what I've learned he went beyond nosey." I watched her closely, "I think he was a bully, even a blackmailer."

She didn't look at all surprised and not in the least guilty. She nodded, "Yes. Nosey people have a habit of learning things that they shouldn't. Let's walk to the office."

"Do you know anyone who might have been affected, shall we say, by his nosiness?"

"Before I answer that, tell me why are you interested in him?"

"I can't say much but I have this friend..." I left it hanging and felt her stiffen. Suddenly I realized how funny it sounded, "No really, I do have this friend and she was harassed by him and I'm trying to help her out." I finished lamely. I realized she probably didn't think the "friend" in my story was real and that I was talking about myself. I started to protest then decided it didn't matter what she thought so I waited.

Jane seemed to be weighing my words and her reply. "In answer to your question, I have some idea about possible blackmail victims but I can't - no let me put it this way - I have absolutely no proof so I won't speculate."

Her words sounded final but the look she gave me told me that if I asked the right questions I might get some sort of answers.

I plunged in, "So what did the Richter's think of him?"

She smiled proudly, my guess was correct, "I don't think they got along at all."

"And Bob your handyman?" I prompted.

"Bob didn't like Slinger either! But I don't know why."

Who else was at the service? "What about Rose Tomson?"

That stopped her. After a minute she said, "I don't think they even knew each other, certainly I've never seen them talking."

"And his neighbor, Carl Reid?"

Jane shook her head, "No idea."

"How about Fred Birch?"

"That was a very strange relationship. I never could figure it out. Do you know how Birch knew Slinger?"

"I know that they worked together at the postal station. Birch still works there. But I don't know how close of friends they were. "

"Ah, that explains it," she said softly.

"Explains what?"

"I didn't know either man well but Fred Birch does come to church regularly, Slinger only occasionally. The strange part is that though they always sat together I have never seen them exchange a single word."

I thought for a moment, "That is weird but I'm not sure any of this helps me. I mean, I want to help my friend and I really do think that blackmail is a direction that the police haven't begun investigating. My problem is that I don't know any of these people so the likelihood of them talking to me is remote."

She paused, "Bob can be difficult, especially lately."

"Any idea why?"

"I don't know. He just seems to be jumpy, you know, on edge."

"Before or after the murder? It sounds like he could be feeling guilty about something."

"Oh, I don't mean to imply that he's the murderer! He's been like this for some time, at least for a few weeks, well before the murder."

"Could it be something to do with blackmail?"

"Possibly."

"Still with him being so jumpy, I don't expect he'd want to talk to me."

"I don't suppose you need a handyman for anything?"

I grinned, "Actually I do! Is he any good? Never mind that doesn't matter, tell him to give me a call." Between working less and paying for a handyman, investigating could prove to be an expensive business.

"I will and I may be able to give you an excuse to talk with the Richter's. I've been clearing out and came across some boxes that the previous vicar must have missed when he sent the stuff over to the historical society. I could give them to you and you could pass them along."

"Won't they wonder why you didn't give the boxes directly to them?"

"Probably, but I am sure you will be able to think up an excuse," she smiled and winked at me, "maybe you are desperate to become a member of their committee."

"I guess I could do some scanning before I deliver them. You know, just as a show of support or help or whatever."

Jane nodded approvingly, "I dusted them off after you called."

"You planned this whole conversation! How did you know what we would decide?"

She smiled smugly, "I didn't, it's just that a big part of my job is evaluating people and I had a feeling we could help each other. Besides I'm always trolling for new parishioners."

I grinned, "Do you knit?" She would fit in very well with our knit group.

She looked startled, "No, but I've always wanted to learn."

"I have some friends who can take care of that. Once this mess is sorted out I'll give you a call when we plan to meet up."

By this time we were in a small room off the side of the main aisle. It looked like it doubled as her office and tearoom. Jane pointed at two cardboard bankers boxes next to the outside door.

"That's odd, I know there were three." She looked around. "Oh, there's the other in the corner." She picked it up and placed it with the others. "They're all yours."

Each box was labeled, School Records 1923-1962, Church Financials 1988-89, and Swann Court 1946-1969. Someone had penciled in Mr. O. Richter and his phone number on the Court box. "I'll help carry them to your car and then I have to run. If I don't unlock the hall door before the Scouts arrive they start playing hide and seek in the gravestones next door," she grinned.

I picked up a box and added a second, they weren't as heavy as I expected, just awkward. We carried them to my car and stowed them in the trunk.

As soon as I got home I opened the trunk.   The court documents might be the most interesting plus it was the lightest box. I brought it up to the living room, leaving the rest behind.

On the way, I noticed that the cat food was gone from the bowl on the back porch so I refilled it. Tom Smooch must be looking for a new home. I'd have to wait for a bit and see how regular his visits were.   Meanwhile, he seemed fine, making his home at least some of the time in my laundry basket.

I had a lot of other things to think about.   Slinger was definitely a bad guy. When a minister calls you nosey, I feel justified in believing the worse.   It would seem his charity knitting and driving really was just a cover. I was glad Minnie was right about him. It made me feel more confident about everything she'd said.

I pulled out my phone and looked again at my photo of the crime scene shots. I downloaded it and made a large print, studying it for a while. Nothing jumped out at me. His knitting project really was a dishcloth and quite a nice one. So it was true that he did knit them for charity. If he was the bad guy, why would he do that?

There was one other thing that I hadn't mentioned to Jack. I was positive it didn't matter and it meant I'd have to reveal my own haphazard approach to knitting. Why on earth would anyone unravel a dishcloth? I'd never do it. Who cares if there are one too many stitches in such a utilitarian item? Maybe Slinger was a perfectionist. Could that have anything to do with his murder?

The bigger questions were the same and I still didn't have any answers, why two different needles and how did the blood get in such an odd place? Then I had a flash of inspiration, it was knit night tomorrow, the perfect opportunity to get some ideas from the group. I'd just have to figure out what questions to ask so that I didn't break my promise to Minnie or Jack.

My talk with Jane also gave me a lot to think about. I was more than just casually interested in this. Not just for Minnie's sake or as the expert witness, by now I was keenly interested in unraveling the puzzle.

For the time being, I'd have to forget about Fred Birch. I didn't know him and couldn't think of a way to casually meet him and yet he sounded the closest link to Slinger. Blackmail and the post office has a nice ring to it and I'd have to think of a way to pursue that, but for now, the Richter's and Bob were easier to approach, if not about murder then at least as blackmail.   Then there was Rose and Carl, they were long shots and so would have to wait.

I decided I really didn't want to hire Bob to do any handiwork. I just didn't like or trust him.   Maybe it was the sweat stained Blue Jays baseball cap he wore pulled low over his eyes or the way he slithered instead of walking, but he gave me the creeps.   When he called I planned to ask my questions and then tell him I decided against having the work done. Meanwhile, I planned tackle the Richter's in the morning.

Back in my living room that evening I opened the court box. Not at all what I expected, it was full of pale blue scribblers, the lined booklets used in school by small children.   There were 10 booklets, each about 30 pages and dated with the months and years covered.   Every page was filled with fine spidery handwriting.   I opened one at random and began reading.   It was notes of a court case.   In 1962, I read how some boys made a dummy out of old clothes and left it on the road at the bottom of their hill then hid behind the bushes to see what would happen.   The first car over the hill was a work truck and the driver swerved to avoid hitting what he thought was a body.   He got out of the cab swearing as the boys giggled in the bushes. Discovering the ruse the driver laughed.   Much to the kid's disappointment, he picked up the dummy, threw it in the back of his truck and drove off.   The case involved the dummy later being found on a busy highway causing a huge traffic snarl.   The boys were caught immediately.   The dummy was wearing one of the boy's coat with his name and phone number on the label sewn inside the collar. I laughed as I turned the page.

After quickly sorting through all the scribblers I saw that there was one book for every two or so years.   I picked up the earliest booklet and found a letter explaining the contents tucked inside.   It was from the granddaughter of Joe Swann. It said that Joe was severely injured in the Second World War and that for the remaining years of his life he   "made it his job" to attend the local courthouse and take notes on the cases. Joe recently passed away and the granddaughter hoped the historical society might make some use of them. It appears Mr. Swann was an extremely dedicated courtroom voyeur.

I began to read only to find it disappointing that none of Swann's personality showed in his writing. The notes were simply a recording of the proceedings. Occasionally there was a comment in the margin such as, "a popular case, the court was full" or " a woman, his mother? wept."

I flipped through a few at random. July 1946, a ration book theft. 1967, house party turned into a drug bust, thinking not much has changed. I decided to scan the documents using a word recognition program. Mr. Swann's handwriting was frequently unreadable by the program so while the machine hummed I made the necessary edits. It was interesting though after the umpteenth traffic summons I was bored and so apparently was Mr. Swann. Pretty soon those cases got a terse entry.

It was still early but I was nodding off from boredom. I decided to multitask and just scan the remaining documents, saving the editing for later. Meanwhile, I would knit a dishcloth to Slinger's pattern, the Picot Edged Diamond Dishcloth. I got out some needles and cotton and cast-on. I was finished in record time then frogged it back about 5 rows, like Slinger's, put a red twist tie to indicate the blood stain where the smooth yarn met the squiggly and carefully put the project in my knit bag before calling it a night, my demonstration for knit night ready and the booklets were scanned.

CHAPTER 16

The next morning was bright and cold. I went for a long walk enjoying the brisk fresh air and hoping to clear my mind. The school grounds were quiet, perhaps a holiday for the kids. When I reached the end of the block I turned the other way, there was no purpose in going by Slinger's house until I thought of some way to approach Carl. He was not the kind of man I wanted to run into unprepared.

I walked the few blocks to Hastings Street and did a little shopping. Some fresh pasta and a few prawns sounded perfect for dinner. I was passing George's office so I sent a text to see if she wanted to stop for a quick coffee. She sent back, "in court. waa." I bought some weatherstripping. If Bob called in person this was my excuse and if not I'd do it myself. By the time I got home I had two new plans. I knew exactly what to say when I phoned Oscar Richter and tonight's knit night would feature a re-enactment of the murder scene.

Neither went according to plan. I was startled when he answered on the first ring, "Is this Oscar Richter?"

"Yes," he answered warily.

"It's Amy Stevens. We met at the church and talked about the historical society?"

There was a long pause. I drummed my fingers on the desk, good grief how many people did he talk to in the last week about this?

Finally, he muttered, "Yeah, I remember."

This was hard work. "I was given some old documents that I was told belong to the historical ...."

He butted in, suddenly angry. "How did you get them and what right have you to handle sensitive documents. That's for the members only!"

I was astonished. He was overreacting, these weren't state secrets and I didn't want to get Jane Harper involved. I tamped down my annoyance choosing to placate, "Oh, I'm sorry. I didn't know. I don't think there is anything confidential, it's just some old court records and..." I heard his sharp intake of breath and hurried on, "I'm really sorry, I had no idea it was wrong and I do plan on becoming a member of the society."

There was silence. Finally, I said, "Mr. Richter?"

"Young lady, I cannot begin to tell you how appalled I am," he spat.

I was stunned, so much for trying to butter him up. "I'm sorry you think so, I was only trying to help."

"They are none of your business. Do not look at the documents, do not even open the box. Just bring them to me," he commanded.

I guessed now was not a good time to tell him they were already scanned in, or that there were actually three boxes full of material. "I'll bring them over when I can," I said and took down his address. He can just wait, I fumed. I'll do it when I'm good and ready. State secrets or not I wasn't jumping to his command.

There was something very wrong with his reaction. Jane never said anything about the files being top secret. In fact, she left them in the church office tea room, not a locked door in the place. Anyone could have seen them.

Remembering the conversation, I realized while he wasn't very welcoming at the beginning, things really went sideways when I mentioned the court box. Did Richter have something against Swann or was it something in the booklets? The more I thought about it the more curious I became.

I put all the booklets back in the box and left it sitting on my ottoman then called Minnie to see if she wanted a ride to knit night at George's.

"Minnie, how are you?"

"Okay," she said faintly.

"Have I caught you at a bad time?"

"No, I'm trying to get an early dinner for Mariko, we have to go to her school tonight for a meeting."

"Oh, I was going to offer you a ride to George's, " I hesitated, "Minnie this is confidential   but I looked at the police file," I heard her quick sharp breath, so I rushed on, "it's okay, I just want to tell you that there was nothing bad in it. The report has the plain facts of what you told the police. And I don't think you have to worry about fingerprints. It said that there were dozens of prints."

Minnie sighed, "Thank you, Amy.   I really appreciate what you're doing."

I assured her I would let her know when anything new came up and rang off.

As I headed out the door my phone rang, call display told me it was Bob.

"Hello," I said tentatively, feeling a coward.

"Yeah, it's Bob from the church. Jane said I should call about some work," he said bluntly.

I was caught off-guard and lost my nerve, "Sorry, the work's already been done," I lied.

"But she only told me yesterday!"

"Well, I'm sorry but there's no work and now I'm late, I have to go.", I hung up abruptly. I knew I was being rude but he made me nervous. Embarrassed and angry I knew any chance of finding out more about Bob was gone. I was turning out to be a pretty terrible investigator.

Hoping my other plan would work out better I drove to George's. It is always entertaining when George hosts knit night. I like to get there early and watch her husband, Tim corral the boys and head out the door. There are hats and gloves and hockey sticks, balls, water bottles, and snacks. They take enough stuff for a whole team even though I know they'll be back long before the knitters have left.

I was glad Minnie wasn't planning on attending. She was still pretty upset and I didn't want to unsettle her anymore. I was afraid my little demonstration for tonight might scare her completely. I planned carefully how to ask for the information I needed without breaking my promises. This was a group of very intelligent ladies, I knew it was going to be difficult to pull the wool over their eyes.

It was a small group tonight, only Tessa, George, Jen and me. That's good, fewer people to swear to secrecy if my demonstrations got out of hand. I began carefully, "I have a theoretical problem I'd like your help with. First I want to show you something."

I pulled the nearly finished dishcloth out of my bag and placed it on my lap, a plastic needle had the stitches on it and a metal needle was lying loose on my lap. Next, I pulled out the bundle of yarn that was attached. I spent some time getting it to look as close to the picture of Slinger's as I remembered. The smooth yarn on the bottom then the twist tie partially buried under the kinked.

When I had it looking as close to the original as I could I began, "Looking at this scene what do you think I'm doing?"

George spoke first, "I don't understand. You're knitting, you just finished unraveling a bit and are ready to begin knitting again. What's the mystery?"

I looked down. She was right of course. I was giving them nothing to work with.

"Sorry, maybe I'll just ask some questions. I held up the mismatched needles. Can you think of any reason someone would knit with a plastic and metal needle? And before you ask, yes, I have the other of the pair in my bag."

"Are they the same size?" Tessa asked.

"Yes." I looked from one to another. No one seemed to have a brain wave.

"Ok, next question, What about the wool at my feet? Pretend that the twist tie is a drop of red wine. How did it get there?" I pointed.

"You spilled your wine without noticing and then began unraveling." George said.

Rats! How was I going to get them to understand that I couldn't have unraveled the yarn, that the wine stain meant I was already dead?

Tessa looked at me squarely, I knew she guessed, "You're up to something Amy. What is it?"

"It's a sort of puzzle and I need you all to help with it," I admitted.

She smiled, "Ah, a puzzle. Go on." George and Jen also nodded.
"So back to the problem. How could the stain get there, under that pile, if I couldn't have done the unraveling?"

Jen asked, "Do you have arthritis in one of your hands?"

"What makes you think that?"

"It might explain the two types of needles. If you prefer metal needles and then get arthritis in one hand you might switch to plastic. Metal is colder and harder to hold. Except that now I think of it that's dumb. On the next row you'd be switching the needle to your bad hand anyway."

And George chimed in "and anyway why not just knit with plastic if you have arthritis?"

Jen smiled, "Good point, it was just an idea."

There was a long pause as we all stared at the needles.

"Ok, so back to the wine stain. Any ideas about that?" I asked.

"Are we sure the same person is the knitter, spilled the wine and did the frogging?" Jen asked.

"Good question. No, I'm not sure. Why, do you have an idea?"

Jen didn't answer, then George said, "What if someone was teaching you a new stitch. They are standing over you and it is their wine that they spill."

I smiled, "Sorry, good answer. I should have made it clearer, the knitter is the wine spiller. But you raise an interesting point. It might be a good idea to consider that the knitter and the un-raveller are different people." I hadn't thought of that, three people at the scene of the crime, Slinger, whoever killed him and a third person who somehow interfered with the knitting. "Frankly if I were the knitter I can't think why anyone else would unravel my work."

"Other than the obvious, of course," Tessa said.

"Something is obvious?"

"Well if the knitter is me!" She laughed, "You know I can never unravel without twisting the stitches on the needle and so I always ask someone else to do it."

"Actually I'd forgotten that annoying habit of yours, " I smiled. "But you're right it is a possible answer."

Privately, I considered it extremely unlikely that it was the correct answer. I would have to check the photo to see if Slinger's stitches were twisted though I didn't think it would matter one way or the other. Knowing the answer wouldn't identify the killer and that was really all that mattered. No one else had any bright ideas so I left it. Far from clarifying the problem, the group made a good case for the possibility of a 3rd person at the scene of the crime.

"I guess if we were to meet up with Inspector Jack we shouldn't talk about spilled wine or your puzzle?" Tessa said sweetly.

"Exactly!" I agreed. I had two more questions for them, "Do any of you know Fred Birch or Carl Reid?" Nothing. "George and Jen, how well do you know Rose?"

George snorted, "Not at all. I have only seen her a couple of times in two years."

Jen laughed, "She cleans your house every week. How is that possible?"

"I leave a note with her cheque detailing what I want done. It is an excellent arrangement, no muss, no fuss, and no time wasted."

Jen shook her head. "Even I don't know her well. She only comes to my house once a month to do some of the heavy work. From time to time I have invited her to share a cup of tea but she always refuses. I think she is a loner. Why do you ask?"

"Oh, I was just thinking about people in the neighborhood and their connections to each other."

George spoke for the group, "Sorry we weren't able to help more."

"That's okay. I'm beginning to think that these questions aren't critical anyway. But let me ask something that is bugging me. If you made a mistake while knitting a dishcloth would you bother to unravel it or just go on?"

"Amy, most people would unravel anything they knit that had a mistake, even if it's a lowly dishrag," George said.

"Everyone except Amy!" Tessa declared.   We were all laughing when Tim and the boys rolled through the front door, a soccer ball landing in the middle of the room. It was time to go.

CHAPTER 17

The minute I opened the back door I knew something was wrong. A cold wind blew down the hall. The kitchen light was on and from where I stood, rooted to the threshold, I saw that my front door was ajar. I didn't hesitate. I turned and ran back to my car, got in, locking the doors at the same time and phoned the police. I turned the engine on with the heat at full blast. I was shivering and not only from the cold.

It seemed like only a few minutes later when there was a knock on the window. I was staring intently at my back door and so screamed in surprise when two shadows covered the car window. Jack rapped on the window. Relief flooded through me as I rolled down the window.

"Are you okay?" Jack asked.

I nodded.

"Stay here. We'll have a look around."

I watched him head up the back stairs, motioning to his partner to go around the front. I lost sight of them both. In a couple of minutes, Jack returned and said that it was okay to come in. I slowly got out of the car and followed him up the stairs. I dreaded entering the house. Jack called to his partner to check the basement while I stood in the kitchen with my coat on and asked weakly, "My studio?"

"Take a deep breath," he said helping me off with my coat, "and don't touch anything in there."

I walked to the doorway. My file cabinet draws were open and papers were scattered. The painting I left on the easel was now on the floor. Someone had put their foot through it. The rest of my works looked untouched.

"There is also a mess in the living room, but the rest looks untouched."

Numbed, I walked down the hall, the box of records was upended and on the floor. All the booklets were thrown around, crumpled and with torn pages. It looked as though someone was furious. I sat in the rocking chair.

Jack looked at me, "What's Tessa's number?"

I handed him my phone.

Within minutes she was making tea. With an effort, I got up and joined her in the kitchen. I slowly came out of my trance. Jack pulled on gloves and went to the living room.

The tea and Tessa's presence worked wonders, I felt better able to cope.

Jack came down the hall carrying the box. "I'm guessing that this is what thief was interested in. I'll take the box and painting now and see if we can get anything from the lab." He placed the box by the back door and went into my studio carefully placing the damaged painting on my easel.

"Can you leave the painting till tomorrow, I promise not to touch it."

He raised an eyebrow but didn't ask me to explain. "Okay. I've blocked your front door, don't use it or even touch it until I can get the fingerprint guys on it. Then you'll need to call and get a new lock."

"Thank you. Really I mean that. I am just so stunned and all I can think about is my art. If I lost that I would lose my income for months. And yet it all looks untouched except for that one painting. Why that one? "

He shrugged, "Maybe it just got in his way or he got frustrated when he couldn't find what he was looking for."

I nodded. That made sense.

"I'm thinking they were searching for a paper. What papers do you keep in the cabinet?"

"Nothing valuable, just bills and sketches. "

"Do you have any idea why anyone would want to go through your papers?"

I shook my head.

"And what's this?" he asked indicating the box under his arm.

"Just some old guy's transcript of old court cases. I got them from the church. They're for the historical society."

"I found ten books. Are any missing?"

"No, there were only ten."

"Until we piece the torn pages back in we won't know for sure if anything is missing. I'll leave the file cabinet for forensics so don't touch anything in your studio. But Amy, you're going to have to think about what could have caused someone to do this. It's not random."

I gasped as I felt the numbness flooding back.

He tried to reassure me, "I don't think it has anything to do with the murder. It's a totally different modus. There was nothing like this at Slingers. Whoever killed Slinger just walked in, did the deed and left. Yours is a straight burglary and pretty amateur. To me, this looks like frustrated searching. I honestly don't think you need to worry. But you do need to think about what you might have that someone wants this badly."

I shivered involuntarily as Tessa laid her hand on my shoulder protectively.

He took the hint. "It's late. I'll drop by in the morning and try to time it with the fingerprint guys."

After he left, Tessa tried to persuade me to go home with her, "I don't like the idea of you here alone. Or I can stay here with you."

"Look I'm fine. Jack secured the front door and I'll bolt and put a chair under the back one." I finally persuaded Tessa to leave. I couldn't tell her the real reason why I needed to be here.

As soon as she was gone I bolted the back door and put the chair under it s promised. Then I took a deep breath and returned to my studio. It's hard to explain how I feel about my art, even to my best friend. My paintings are like my children. If I was vulnerable after the burglary, they were even more so. Without touching anything I carefully examined what I could. Except for the damaged one they were untouched. This, as nothing else could have, convinced me that the break-in was non-threatening. The burglar was looking for something and became angry and frustrated but not at me personally, of that I was sure. Otherwise, they must know that the one way to harm or intimidate me would be to destroy my art, not just one unfinished painting.

The wrecked canvas stared back at me from the easel. It was the ferrets. Two sleek animals on a turquoise blanket. Why would someone so thoroughly destroy it? To send a message? If so, I wasn't smart enough to understand.

Eventually, I went to bed. Sleep eluded me and I lay for a long time trying to make sense of the break-in. I was puzzled and angry. I must have something that someone wanted very badly. But there was nothing. The court files? That didn't make sense. They were a matter of public record. And who knew I had them? Tired and confused I finally slept.

The forensics team arrived early, without Jack. They were efficient as they dusted for fingerprints found mine and told me the burglar had worn gloves. They packaged up the damaged painting. I was quite happy not to have to look at it anymore.

I asked what they thought of the theft. They shook their heads and referred me to the Inspector. As soon as they left I put my paperwork back in the file cabinet. As far as I could tell nothing was missing. At noon, the locksmith showed up and installed new locks on the front and back doors and an electronic entry on the basement door. I'd never locked the basement before now. There was nothing worth stealing. Dirty laundry, canned fruit? Now I felt vulnerable. I wanted security and my new locks gave me that.

I spent the afternoon painting backgrounds, it was relaxing and helped me think.

Are Slinger's death, Minnie's blackmail and now my break-in connected? Of course, my mind screamed! But could I make a case that they weren't? First, the burglary, if it was some kids looking for quick resale electronics they were doomed to disappointment. I had nothing worth stealing. The TV was still on the wall and untouched. My laptop was an older model and lay on the top of the file cabinet. It hadn't even been opened, the fingerprint guys told me. So Jack must be right, it wasn't random. So what was the connection?

Could someone have found out that I was a consulting with the police? Was I somehow a threat because of that? I double checked but my knotting bag was untouched and sitting where I had left it before the burglary. That took me back to the knitting angle and that seemed ludicrous. It was more likely that they looking for something specific and got angry when they couldn't find it. Jack said he thought it was papers and that made sense as my immediate impression of the mess in the living room and studio was of the papers and the booklet pages, crumpled and torn, ripped out in frustrated anger.

Jack now had the box of original booklets but I still had the scanned pages on my computer. Should I finish the editing work I started the other night? Would I find some clue? Or should I leave it to the police? Jack would let me know soon enough if something were missing. Then the scanned documents would be critical, if not it might be a waste of time to read through the material, duplicating the work of the police.

I was sure that somehow this was the connection I needed, the connection between blackmail and murder. Papers, maybe even these booklets must be the link. Perhaps my burglar was a blackmail victim who was now scared knowing that with Slinger dead his or her secret would be exposed once these booklets or any other of the historical documents to which Slinger had access were made public.

I really wanted to tell Jack about the blackmail, positive it was a lead he hadn't explored. But I kept my promise to Minnie.

I worked steadily till my back ached slightly and I realized I was starving. I made a sandwich and ate it quickly before going back to work. Slowly I relaxed. Painting for me is all consuming. It is like meditation. By the time the light started to fail I made a very good start on a sketch for September, a fish tank with a school of clown fish and added a sand castle in the bottom of the tank. The fish were coming along too. I painted them swimming towards me like they would swim right into my arms. I also came up with a new idea and a question for Jack.

Late in the day, I called him. He sounded distracted and I could hear him talking to another person half covering the phone. "Hi Amy, sorry I didn't make it by. I don't have anything to tell you yet."

"I thought as much. No problem. I've been thinking. Did the coroner say anything about whether the killer was a man or woman?"

"Why do you want to know?"

"Just curious."

I could hear the wariness in his voice as he replied, "The needle was dull as you know but it was metal and one good shove could have done it. The pathologist said male or a strong female. And forensics said it couldn't have been wiped after it was used."

So the killer was wearing gloves, as did my burglar. That was interesting but it was winter and everyone wore gloves. "Did you find out how long it might have taken him to die?"

"Short. Way too short to do any knitting."

"Thanks, bye"

"Wait a minute, what's this about?"

"Just your expert witness mulling over things. I know you're busy so I'll let you go. "

I could feel his frown over the line.

"Is this about your friend?"

I wasn't even thinking about Minnie. Horrified I hoped I hadn't refocussed his thoughts on her. "No, no it's nothing to do with her. It was just to do with the knitting. Sorry, I have to go," I said and rang off before he could question me further.

CHAPTER 18

It was time to put my newest idea to the test. I walked to my favorite vegetable market. At this time of year, most of the produce was from other countries but it still has the feel of a summertime Farmers Market. Everything always looks so good. Bright colors, piled high. I bought an acorn squash, a mini watermelon, and some apples. My bags were awkward and heavy and I was kicking myself for not bringing the car. As I left the market one of the plastic handles slipped and I managed to catch my fruit before it rolled away. As I straightened I caught sight of Carl, Slinger's next door neighbor. He was at the cafe next door having coffee with another man. I could only see the back of the other man's head but he looked familiar. Of course, the uniform. It was Fred Birch, the guy Slinger worked with before he retired. How did the two men know each other? At the memorial service, I was sure they hadn't acknowledged one another. I found a ledge and set my bags on it to relieve the weight while I studied the men. I was too far away to hear anything and was reluctant to move any closer for fear they would notice me. Their discussion was heated with Carl doing most of the talking. It looked like Carl was accusing Birch, pointing at him repeatedly. Suddenly Birch rose, dumped his coffee cup in the garbage and stomped away. Carl wore a satisfied smile on his face as he continued to sip his drink. Birch was coming my way so I leaned over fiddling with my bags as he sped past. He looked angry and even a little shaken. I waited a minute and left taking a different route.

This was something positive to tell Jack that couldn't lead back to Minnie. When I got home I called and it went directly to voicemail. I didn't bother to leave a message, better to tell him in person.

I washed the fruit and vegetables and left them drying on the kitchen counter. I steamed some fish and gyoza for dinner and ate quickly. Carl Reid and Fred Birch, my list of possible blackmail victims was getting quite long. There was Bob Strauss, Oscar and Camellia Richter and Rose Tomson. To the list, I also added my burglar though quite probably he or she was already on the list. Too many people and not enough clues. How was I ever going to eliminate any of them?

I read somewhere that if you smash a watermelon it looks like a crushed skull. That gave me the idea to test just how easy it is to poke a knitting needle into a human neck or in my case a watermelon. It was probably a stupid experiment but if I could prove, at least in my own mind, that an older woman didn't have the strength to do it I could scratch three names from my list. Four, if I included Minnie.

I took out the half knitted dishrag and stared at it. No flashes of brilliance came so I stuffed it back in my knitting bag and took out the loose No. 6 metal needle. I really don't like knitting with metal needles, I'm a bamboo girl myself. Since the murder, I planned to donate all my old metal sets. It was pure chance that I owned a pair that looked very much like the one used to kill Slinger.

Assuming things could get messy, I got out an old beach towel and spread it on the kitchen table. I placed the watermelon on the towel and tried to spear it with the needle. It rolled away. Mr. Slinger didn't roll away, I cringed, my thoughts gruesome.

I held the melon down with one hand and skewered with the other. The needle went in easily coming out the other side. Did the needle go right through Slinger's neck? I had no idea. Did the photos show blood on the back of the chair? None of the shots were that detailed. To find out for sure I'd have to ask Jack.

I sat back and considered the watermelon. Skewering it was too easy. A human neck couldn't be that easy.

I found that the acorn squash had a much tougher skin. My hand slipped on the needle and the squash skittered off the table. Thankfully it didn't crack open. I got out my rubber gloves for traction and pulled the table over against the wall. Placing the towel and squash on it, I called "En Garde!" and skewered. With a better grip and two hands, the needle went through the squash, out the other side and made a neat little hole in the drywall. I didn't know whether to laugh or cry.

All my experiment proved was that any of the suspects, including Minnie, could have done the murder; a knitting needle is a formidable weapon. My hope of eliminating anyone was dashed and the only thing I had to show for it was a hole in my kitchen wall.

I cut the squash and put it in the oven to roast. Dicing the melon, I put it in the freezer for smoothies. I felt better once the evidence of my silly experiment was gone. The towel was splattered so I took it downstairs to start a load of wash.

I stuffed it into the machine and picked up the basket. Near the bottom was my favourite dish towel, the one I'd noticed before. It had a dirty stain on it, like paint. I couldn't remember how it happened but I am a messy painter and dabs seem to show up in weird places so I put it in a pail of cold water to soak. By the time I got upstairs I was on edge. Maybe it was the leftover feelings of guilt from a wasted evening but I needed to get out of the house and do something completely different. I knew that Claire was back in town so I called her.

Claire is wickedly funny and the stories she tells about her travels and clients are endlessly entertaining. When we are together I feel like I'm living in a People magazine. The diversion of her world was exactly what I needed. She answered on the first ring sounding a bit groggy. "Oh I'm sorry did I wake you?" Oops, I knew I had.

"What time is it? "

"Just after 9, go back to sleep and call me in the morning."

"No, that's ok, I'm awake. I need to get up anyway and have something to eat. Otherwise, I won't sleep through the night."

"I was hoping you'd say that, what do you feel like? A Pub?"

"You have got to be kidding!"

"Sorry, I forgot."

"I thought Britain was bad, but no, the Welsh, darlings though they are, actually eat French fry sandwiches."

I laughed.

"I'm not kidding. They have the nutritional value of a tennis ball. If I see another chip I will scream."

"How about Tokyo Sam's?"

"Give me 20 minutes and I'll meet you there."

Perfect. Sam's wasn't far from my house. I put the squash on the counter to cool and decided to walk. It was overcast so I grabbed an umbrella, standard outdoor gear for Port Oxford. Claire and I arrived at the same time. We exchanged hugs and settled into a low table booth.

I ordered the tuna tataki appetizer and watched as Claire plowed her way through an enormous bowl of spicy salmon don.

Claire is 37 and looks much younger. She spends a lot of time and energy on her appearance. I like her a lot or I would call her vain. She has brown curly hair that she has professionally straightened every 6 months. I've seen pictures of her and love her with curls. Why is it that every woman wants the kind of hair they weren't born with?

Claire finally pushed her bowl away, "God I needed that!"

"You say that every time you come back from anywhere."

"I know. I love travel food, though by the time I get home all I want is the opposite of what I have just eaten. If I was just back from Japan we'd be having hamburgers and fries," she admitted, "so tell me what's been going on in Port Oxford."

I told her about knit night and how we were interrupted by the police, then about Mr. Slinger, the knitting angle, the memorial service and the burglary. I didn't tell her about Minnie's involvement.

"Who is investigating?" she asked.

"His name is Jack Sommerville."

Claire smiled, "Ah, you mean Jackson."

"Well, yes, do you know him?"

"We go way back," she said with a dreamy look in her eye.

I felt my heart skip a beat. It sounded as though Claire knew Jack and I mean really knew him. This was not good news.

"He's gorgeous isn't he?" she said wistfully.

I nodded.

"Hm, now that I'm back in town I'll have to give him a call."

"I'm sure he'd like that," I said stiffly.

I walked home slowly. So that was the end of that. Not that there was ever much, to begin with. He was a nice man doing his job and that was all. I needed to tell him about the argument between Carl Reid and Fred Birch. If I called now chances were it would go to voicemail. My luck was in, this time I left a message about the encounter between the two men. I even told him he didn't need to call back. I hoped he'd take the hint, I didn't want to talk to him right now. But I did want him to act. It was over a week since the murder and nothing seemed to be happening. Would the argument between Reid and Birch be enough to suggest blackmail as a lead?

I slept soundly. By the morning I knew that in the eyes of the police an argument did not equal blackmail so I decided to tackle the Richter's. There was something very odd about the way they behaved at the service, a kind of timid relief. It was not the kind of reaction to expect when a colleague dies. And my phone call with Oscar Richter was bizarre and needed an explanation.

Assuming that either Mr. or Mrs. Richter or both of them, were blackmail victims how could I find out for sure? How do you get a blackmail victim to confess? Getting Minnie to say anything was like pulling teeth and Minnie was a good friend. What would it take for strangers to unburden themselves? As I worked in my studio I turned it over in my mind and ended up sketching a rabbit that looked demonic. After lunch I scrutinized the canvas knowing I would have to scrap the whole thing and start again. Angry with myself I got on my coat and went for a walk. I needed milk and there was a corner store just past the church. The obvious route to investigating Oscar Richter was through the historical committee so a look at the church bulletin board should give me information on their meetings. And as I wasn't keen on confronting Oscar on his own a committee meeting would be a safe place. He was bound to be annoyed when I told him his precious box was now in the hands of the police.

It was a beautiful day and getting out of the house felt wonderful. I walked briskly the long way around to the store and got the milk. Coming back I entered the church through the side door. It was quiet and serene. The honey colored stone was warm and calming.

I couldn't see anyone around so I left via the front door where the notice board hangs. There were lots of 'for sale' notices and the scouts were having a manure sale (I hoped not in the churchyard). Finally, I found a list of phone numbers, one was for the historical committee. I made a note of the number.

I could hear sounds coming from behind the church. Looking for Jane I rounded the corner and saw Bob raking leaves. I know I tend to think of some people in terms of animals but he really did look like a small weasel or ferret. A narrow face, large high forehead with a thin brush of salt and pepper hair. Small ears. I shook my head, maybe I just had ferrets on the brain. He was talking quietly to himself. I couldn't hear what he was saying but he did not look happy.

I should have turned away but impulsively, I said, "Hi," and walked closer.

"What do you want?" He raised his rake, startled.

"Sorry, I didn't mean to surprise you." I took a step back, eyeing the rake.

"I'm busy," he said turning his back while pulling his cap lower over his forehead.

I quickly retraced my steps. Once out of sight, I breathed much easier. He was scary and it was foolish of me to approach him without a plan. But just because he didn't like to be interrupted didn't mean he killed anyone. On the other hand, his behavior put him at the top of my list of suspects.

I made my way slowly home frustrated that I'd let him frighten me into running away. Avoiding unpleasant people made investigating impossible. And, worse, it didn't look like there'd be another, less threatening opportunity to talk with him. I decided to turn my attention to Oscar Richter and the Historical Committee.

CHAPTER 19

The best opportunity to talk to Richter was at one of the historical committee meetings. It would be on neutral territory. Not like my encounter with Bob Strauss, alone and him with a potential weapon in his hand. I know a rake, but still. The odds of meeting up with Richter at a committee meeting were good but not perfect. But it was the best plan I cold come up with.

I hesitated before calling the historical committee, before I made personal contact I wanted to know what the committee actually did. At least then I'd have a reason for approaching him. So before calling the coordinator I decided to go to the library for background information. I even had the perfect cover story.

There is something about libraries that I love. The dusty smell and the hush. But it was a long time since I'd been inside a library.

When I went up the steps and opened the door I was surprised. Things had changed. There was noise, all kinds of sounds and people talking in regular voices, no whispering. The librarian was reassuringly unchanged, grey haired and kindly. Her half glasses slipping down her nose, she sat at her desk amidst balloons and banners proclaiming "Spring into Reading!"

"Excuse me," I whispered. "Can you tell me where I would find some historical documents about Port Oxford?"

"What exactly are you looking for" she whispered back with a twinkle, adding in her regular voice, "You know you don't have to whisper."

I smiled, "Old habit. I'm looking for some photos of buildings and maybe a local history if there is such a thing. My Grandfather was a builder and I understand that he built a lot of the houses around here. I want to see if I can find anything about him or if the city's historical committee might have something."

PAST

"Here, I'll show you." She led the way pass an area filled with very small children nestled among plush cushions. A young woman was reading from a large picture book. It was story time and the two-year-olds were listening but restless.

"What better way for children to spend the day than in the quiet," I rolled my eyes toward the growing mayhem, "of the library."

"I'm afraid that quiet and library are no longer synonymous." She looked over at the smiling faces and waved at them, "And that's a good thing." She pointed to a shelf with a sign above it, "I think you'll find everything we have in this area. Port Oxford: Facts, Figures, and Fotos." Someone had a sense of humor. "This area is maintained by our Historical Society. Actually, they are meeting here next Saturday, perhaps you could join them."

I hedged, "I'll see, I'll have to check my calendar."

She smiled, "I'll make a note of the date and time for you. And what's your name? Just in case you come they'll want to make sure they have plenty of coffee and cookies."

Hooked and reeled in by a pro, before I knew it I'd be volunteering for a spot on the Board. Now I'd have to show up. But how could I ensure Richter would also be there. I watched the librarian return to her desk.

Turning to the shelf I saw a meagre selection of material. I opened a large scrapbook, The Port Oxford Historical Review.

It was clearly a work in progress, photocopies of articles and pictures were taped inside. A notice tucked inside the cover noted that this was a mock-up of a book, due out next year and asked for input from readers.

I began turning the pages and found old prints of the city when the roads were still dirt and the tallest building was the hotel, 2 stories with a false front. There were lists of businesses and photos of civic officials planting trees and kissing babies. Maps of the city showed the growth over the years and an artist's drawn plans showed business locations in tiny print. It was fascinating. I found my Grandfather's building company. It was now the site of a pharmacy. There were ads from local business with one I knew that was still in business. The Scottish Butcher looked the same now as it did then and was still in the same location, even the ham hanging in the window probably hadn't changed.

At the back of the book was a list of society members and there he was, Frank Slinger along with Jane Harper (Rev.) and Mr. and Mrs. O. Richter among at least a dozen other names, including Minerva Grant. "Oh No!" I gasped loudly. I looked around but no one seemed to have noticed.

Why hadn't Minnie told me she was a member? The list wasn't dated but the cover note said that the work began just over two years previously. It was reasonable to assume that all of them were members for at least that long. She must know Slinger better than she led me to believe. I closed the book, shaking. Minnie was a good person, I knew that, but even good people can do something bad, even criminal. Suddenly I was seeing her as a stranger.

I needed to think and this wasn't the place. Story time was now a sing-a-long and getting louder and I needed peace and quiet. I walked slowly back home. From one corner of my porch I could just see a scrap of Minnie's lawn. It was a long way away on the other side of the schoolyard so I couldn't see any detail, couldn't even tell if the lights were on. If I turned and looked farther up her street I could see Slinger's house, dark as a tomb. I sat on my porch and stared at each of them in turn until it got too cold, then I went inside.

Tom was scratching at the back door so I let him in. "Hey big guy, you're looking a little trimmer than last time I saw you," I crouched to pat him. "Let's see what I have for you?" We shared leftovers from the fridge. I was supposed to go out with Claire again but I called and told her I was maybe coming down with something. She was full of concern. I finally convinced her I was tired but that I'd be fine. In a way it was true. I was tired, tired of thinking, tired of worrying and definitely too tired to tackle Minnie or dodge the Claire/Jack situation.

I took a long bath with lots of lavender scented bubbles. I lay soaking and finally relaxed as I considered my feelings for Jack. I ran through every encounter and every conversation in my head and knew in my bones that there was nothing there. He'd never said or done anything to suggest that I was anything more than a witness. Sure, he dropped over that one time to see the basement and that might not have been strictly necessary. On the other hand it did make a certain amount of sense. And the meeting at the coffee shop was simply convenient for him, certainly not a date. Really it all came down to Tessa's suggestion that he was gorgeous and then her scuttling everyone out of the house that first night. Jen hadn't helped calling our appointment a date.

"This is really embarrassing," I said to the bathroom and Tom who was sleeping on the mat. "I'm old enough to know better." Reviewing my own behavior I felt I hadn't exposed my feelings too much. It was true that I manoeuvred to change into something nice that first night – or rather Tessa bulldozed me. After that I'd worn a variety of mostly painting clothes, sad but true. And I couldn't remember saying anything revealing in our conversations. All in all I felt better.

Maybe he was unaware of my interest. Men don't notice things like that, I told myself. Tom rolled over; obviously he agreed.

Convincing myself of Minnie's innocence was harder. I could not reconcile her failure to tell me about her involvement in the Historical Society with Slinger. After a long time, when my fingers were all prune-y, I went to bed.

I woke up to sunlight streaming in through the cracks in my curtains. After my long sleep I felt rested and motivated. Jane's invitation to church beckoned on this beautiful, almost spring-like day. I felt like a little girl as I selected a hat, choosing a pale lavender cloche I knit the previous year and walked in the bright sunshine the few blocks to the morning service. It seemed everyone had the same idea, there was a steady stream of people climbing the stairs of the church.

I couldn't remember the last time I'd been to a Sunday church service. Today it felt welcoming, warmed from the sunshine streaming through the stained glass. I looked at the congregation, picking out the Richter's and Bob, who was by himself at the side with a rag in one hand and his cap pulled low. He met my eyes briefly and turned quickly to slide away. It did not appear that any of the other people from the memorial were here. Minnie sat alone at the end of a pew about half way up the aisle. I slid in next to her.

She looked at me and smiled vaguely. Reassured I reached across and squeezed her hand.

The Reverend Harper did a good job. The service was well paced and her sermon interesting. There was a guitar playing interlude and soon it was over. It was satisfying, interesting and even fun.

I wanted to talk with the Reverend Jane and turned to ask Minnie to come with me only to find she'd slipped away. Jane crossed the aisle to join me.

"Nice to see you again," she said taking Minnie's seat.

"I really liked the service."

Jane smiled, "You sound surprised."

I hesitated.

"Not to worry, it's my job to encourage people to give us a try," she said.

"I will admit this is a pleasant way to spend a Sunday morning, so you may see me here again."

"I hope so but no pressure." Her smile turned to a frown as she spotted Bob grimly making his way towards us.

I followed her eyes, "That reminds me," I said urgently, "you need to have a chat with Bob. I came to the church a few days ago and he was very rude. I hope he isn't like that with everyone."

She shook her head, "I can't understand it. He's changed. Bob has always been shy but in the last few weeks he's sullen one minute and anxious the next. I really have to sit down with him and see what the problem is."

"Ok and forget about the handyman idea. He called but it wasn't a good time and I'm not sure it was a good idea anyway. Maybe now would be a good time for your heart to heart with him," I said and slipped out of the pew.

I spotted the Richter's with Minnie at the front door of the church. Feeling protective, like a mother hen when her chick wanders off, I hurried over.

Minnie stood between the couple. Her peaceful air had vanished, now everything about her drooped. Her fingers nervously plucked at her handbag. I swooped in and put my arm around her, drawing her away. "Minnie dear, Mr. and Mrs. Richter, how are you?" I clucked brightly.

Minnie looked at me gratefully and Mr. Richter took his wife by the elbow and turned to go as he mumbled, "Fine."

"Actually you're just the people I was looking for. Can you tell me a little about genealogy? My family were early settlers in the area and I wondered if you had any information about them." My trip to the library had roused my curiosity and provided the perfect approach to the Richters.

Mrs. Richter smiled and turning to her husband said, "We have lots of information. Don't we dear?"

Mr. Richter sneered, "We have the parish records of course but as I have never seen you at church I doubt that your family would be in them."

"Frankly, I have no idea but didn't you say that you also have the city records?"

"Yes, but you'll have to wait till it's all online."

His wife seemed to realize he was being rather rude. She patted his sleeve, murmuring, "If you want to drop the names of your ancestors at our house we can see if we have anything when we get the chance."

I made a note of their address.

Mr. Richter stared at me with contempt, "I don't know why I should answer any of your questions, you still haven't returned that box of records!"

"I can't." I replied calmly. "Didn't you hear? The police have them,"

Oscar Richter turned white so fast I thought he was going to faint. His wife looked on bewildered. "What are you both talking about? What box?" Camilla asked.

So she didn't know. Minnie who had silently followed the exchange was also surprised. "I had a break-in and it was impossible to know what the thief wanted so the police took a few things including the box." I watched Oscar closely as I added, "I think they wanted to study them."

His color went from white to grey. There was no question in my mind, Oscar Richter was terrified of something in the box. He took his wife's elbow and pushed her out the door.

I looked after them speculatively. Since he didn't know the police had the box it proved for sure that he couldn't be the burglar. I could rule out his wife as well, she hadn't even known the box existed. Minnie was dazed as I walked her to her car. "What was that all about?" she asked "I didn't know you'd been burgled!"

"It's nothing to do with you. Really!'" I smiled reassuringly. "It's just something I'm working on."

"Are you sure?" she asked faintly. "I just can't seem to shake the feeling of doom."

"Positive. Minnie, you have to stop worrying.You look exhausted. Are you okay to drive?"

"I'm fine."

"I'll tell you what, I'll bring something over and we can share an early dinner. Meanwhile you go put your feet up and have a rest."

She nodded and I watched as she drove away. Dinner would also give me the chance to ask her about her membership in the historical society.

I walked slowly up the street. On the far side of the road Camellia stood next to a car. Near her, Oscar was in the midst of an argument with a third person who I couldn't quite see. As I got closer I realized it was Rose.

I slowed to eavesdrop. Rose was furious, shouting at Oscar to leave Camellia alone, "She hasn't done anything, she never has done anything. Abuse! That's what it is! That's what you're doing! "

Camellia groaned slumping against the car.

Rose screamed at Oscar, "Now look what you've done!"

"Me! It's you who said it. You stay out of it, Rose!" Oscar seethed. Where before he was gray, now he was scarlet.

Rose stood, clenching and unclenching her fists.

"Get in the car, Camellia," he commanded.

As Camellia meekly obeyed, Rose shouted, "bastard" and stalked away. I watched as they all drove away. It was clear that Rose knew both of the Richter's very well. Here was another connection between people who were at the memorial. Could their argument have something to do with Slinger? First I'd need to find out what the connection was between the three of them. Maybe Minnie could help with that too.

CHAPTER 20

I dug a macaroni and cheese from the freezer, loaded it in the car and drove over to Minnie's via the back lane, passing Slinger's house. There were no lights on, no 'for sale' sign and the garage door was closed. The houses on both sides were also dark. I looked closely at Carl's windows but didn't see any twitching curtains.

Suddenly I had an 'Ah-ha' (AHA) moment and nearly ran into a hydro pole. Why hadn't I asked the question before? A prime reason people are murdered is greed. Who benefits? I'd been so intent on the blackmail aspect I was neglecting this basic question. By this time the police must have been able to trace the relatives and maybe even found a will.

I parked behind Minnie's car and brought the food into her house. Mariko let me in and the three of us had a quiet meal. Afterwards Minnie looked much better even relaxed. Mariko eyed me gratefully and left to do homework.

"Minnie," I asked as we washed the dishes, "do you know Rose Tomson?"

"No. Who is she?"

"Never mind, I saw her at church and wondered if you knew her. How about any of Slinger's relatives? I'm thinking of his will, if he had one."

"Sorry, I don't know anything about his family."

She said it offhand but I wondered again if she was hiding something. "But you've known him for a long time. I mean you were on the historical committee together," I said watching her closely.

Her answer was casual, "Yes but only for a few years and I never liked him so I kept my distance. He was most unpleasant, always sneering and being nasty to people."

Her answer was such an innocent explanation I felt guilty for my suspicions. I relaxed leaning against the counter while drying my hands, "I'm just wondering if money might be a motive for the killing."

"How do you mean?"

"Well, the house and Chevy alone are worth a fair amount to whoever stands to inherit. Greed is a common motive. "

She seemed cheered by the thought, "Do you really think so?"

"You know what they say, 'cherche le cash'" I said giving her a hug as I left to go home.

Following the money sounded easy. Surely the police would be investigating whoever stood to inherit. The other money angle, the blackmail was proving to be a huge hurdle that I just couldn't seem to surmount. Of course by avoiding half the suspects I wasn't doing myself any favors. Of all of them Mrs. Richter seemed the mostly likely to let something slip to a complete stranger and she was by far the least scary. I had her address, maybe if I showed up one day when Oscar was out she would invite me in for a chat. I'd do a drive-by and if their car was gone take a chance.

Meanwhile I had a living to make, a basset hound for June named Ben. His liquid eyes were begging to be painted but I couldn't concentrate. I looked around the studio and saw the rabbit I had scrubbed the other day. It looked just as bad now as then so I made it disappear under a coat of gesso. Splashing gesso around made me feel better. I cleaned up and by teatime I was in my car. The Richter's live only a few blocks away but having my car meant I could make a quick getaway. I really did not want to run into the Mr.

Their house was perfect. Too perfect. The lawn was so manicured it looked fake. I did a double take to check. It was real but the flowers in the window boxes were plastic. The whole place looked like an oversized dollhouse.

I scanned the street and didn't see their car. Hoping for the best, I rang the bell. Mrs. Richter answered immediately, almost like she was waiting for someone. I said as much, "Hello, I hope I'm not interrupting you?"

"No," she said vaguely looking past me. I couldn't take my eyes off her. She was dressed like a caricature from a British mystery in a matching beige twinset and tweed skirt. If she'd been carrying secateurs I would have run for my car.

Pulling myself together I said brightly, "I thought I would drop off the stuff about my family." I held up the envelope of the hastily gathered information about my grandparents that was the excuse for the visit. Mechanically she reached out to take the papers but I held on, "I'll need to give you a bit more detail than is in here." She didn't respond to my subtle hint. Steeling myself I said boldly, "Is there any chance I could come in for a chat?" I'd come this far and I wasn't going home without something,

That startled her. "Now?"

"Oh, that would be lovely!" I exclaimed as I slipped through the door.

Almost immediately I wished I hadn't. I was standing in a short hall. On my left was a small table covered by a plastic doily. A large brown vase filled with more fake flowers sat in the centre. I could see into the living room. The lamps were encased in plastic covers, every cushion was perfectly plumped and placed. I doubt the room was ever used it was so uninviting.

Camellia didn't seem to know what to do, I wondered if I was the first visitor she'd ever entertained. Uncertainly she turned in the direction of the living room. Betting that the kitchen would be a better setting for the kind of conversation I hoped would ensue, I suggested, "Why don't we sit in your kitchen it's so much more cosy for a chat and a cup of tea?"

She was bowled over by my boldness but so was I. So far so good. I followed her down the hall. The kitchen was a small square. A table stood under the net curtained window. The countertops were fake wood and the walls were papered in a garish orange and yellow wallpaper. Plastic placemats on the formica table were reminiscent of the 50's. It smelled faintly of bleach. At least I knew it was clean.

"How long have you lived here?"

She filled the kettle, less vague as she went about this ordinary task. "35 years."

"You have a lovely home." I lied, "so cosy. Is Mr. Richter not at home?"

"No, he's gone to the store."

Not a lot of time, I guessed. "With your work for the historical society you must know a lot about the neighborhood."

"Oscar does. I only help with the note taking and such."

When she finally poured the tea it tasted faintly of chlorine. Even the boxed cookies she laid out looked bleached.

I sipped. "So, 35 years. And how long have you been working with the historical committee?"

"Actually Oscar started it. It must be 10 years ago. "

"How did it start?" Conversation was getting easier, like a rusty engine, she just needed a little help getting started.

"It was really the last vicar, Reverend Blatherwick. He came from Scotland just after the war. You know, he never lost his brogue," she said as though this was the most interesting fact about him, her voice trailing off.

"Was he interested in history?" I prodded gently.

"What? Oh, not really. But other people started to be interested in genealogy and kept bothering him. He said it was taking up too much of his time so he asked Oscar if he would do something with all the records."

"Does Oscar know a lot about computers?"

"He's very good at organizing things. He set up an email address and then a website. After that the requests started coming in."

"Gosh, that sounds like a lot of work. How many would you handle in a month?"

"I never do any of the computer work I leave that to Oscar. I guess at the beginning about 3 or 4 a month, now it seems a bit less. A lot of the information is already on other websites, I think."

A regular avalanche. I tried to sound sincere, "that is just wonderful, it is so nice of you to give back to the community in this way." Camellia flushed, flattered.

"Is the work finished? Are all the records on the internet now?"

"No, Oscar just doesn't have time to do it all, that was supposed to be Frank's job. I don't know who we'll get now that he is gone."

I seized the chance, if this was something Slinger was involved in then there was a good chance I could find out what he was doing just before he died so I offered, "I could help out if you like."

She looked at me as though I were an alien, "You know how to do that kind of thing?"

"Yes, a bit anyway." I decided to downplay my expertise, I didn't want this to become a full time job.   "Do you know what Frank was working on recently."

"I have no idea, you'll have to talk to Oscar."

She did not want to talk about Frank and I did not want to talk to Oscar.   I needed information so I tried again, "How long has Frank been doing the work?"

"Frank only ever helped a bit and only in the last couple of years. Oscar really had to do it all and yet Frank wanted his name on the papers just like Oscar."

"Oscar must have been annoyed by that."

She looked surprised at the idea, then added meditatively, "He would be ever so cross about Frank but it seems like recently, at the meetings, he was agreeing to everything Frank said."

She sounded puzzled by this behavior. I realized I probably knew the answer. Oscar was a blackmail victim, not his wife and he hadn't told her.   With a feeling of disappointment I realized that she wasn't going to be of any help to me after all, I'd still have to talk with Oscar and I couldn't see that going well.

"That does sound odd. You don't know what it was that made Oscar so mad at Frank?" I tried one last time.

"No I don't. I'm so glad he won't be working with us anymore." She looked quite stricken as she realized what she said. "Oh dear, I didn't mean, I mean…"

"I sympathize. It must have been hard to work on a committee with someone who abused his position."

She shot up out of her seat, wringing her hands and turning a deep red crying, "Look at the time, I really must be…I mean Oscar will be home any moment and I haven't even begun to get his dinner ready."

Her reaction startled me, she looked terrified. We were having a nice conversation, if slightly one sided, and then something set her off.
"I'm sorry if I upset you. I really have no idea why… " I let the sentence hang hoping she might fill in the blank. She didn't. Instead she took my unfinished cup and stood with her back to me huddled over the sink. I could see she was shaking. The message was clear, my time was over.

As I left I thanked her for the tea and assured her I would get in touch with Oscar.

"You won't tell him," she pleaded wringing her hands roughly, she sounded terrified of her husband.

"I don't know what you mean but I promise I won't even say that I've been to see you. Okay?"

That seemed to calm her so I slipped past her and out the door, my envelope still clutched in my hand. I took a deep breath of fresh air, it smelled so good and hurried to my car. On the way home I thought about our discussion, trying to recreate it word by word. Something set her off. She might have just noticed the time and worried Oscar would show up but her reaction was awfully extreme. Then I remembered Rose's venom towards Oscar. Maybe Rose was right and Camellia was scared of Oscar. Blast! I'd forgotten to ask how they knew Rose.

Sleuthing was proving to be hard work. I needed a sounding board. Certainly not Minnie, it would have to be someone else. My promise to Minnie was one I could no longer keep. On the theory it was easier to beg forgiveness than ask for permission I decided to talk with Tessa. She didn't pick up when I called so I left her a message suggesting we meet for lunch or dinner the next day.

CHAPTER 21

I ate dinner while making a list of what I knew about the murder and the people involved. It was pretty vague but it did help to order my thoughts for when I could talk with Tessa.

Later that evening, watching an English murder mystery I realized how different it was in real life. Without access to the police information I was sleuthing in the dark. And it was going to be even more difficult as long as I was avoiding the investigating inspector. But I still had the photo of the crime scene shots, another look might turn up something new.

I downloaded the photo and enlarged it till it covered 4 sheets of paper. I printed it off in colour and taped the sheets together spreading it out on the ottoman with my knitting light shining on it. The first thing I noticed was how different my photo looked compared to the original. They were glossy while mine was dull. Without the shine I could see more detail which was weird because it really was a copy of a copy.

Frank looked very comfortable, except for the needle. I was convinced that he was the knitter, that this wasn't some elaborate charade to confuse the police. I added my original questions to the list.

Question: Why would someone use two different knitting needles?
I'd already told the Inspector the most obvious reason. Was there any other? Some patterns use different needles for an effect. But there was nothing like that in this pattern, so that couldn't be the reason. Jen's explanation was original but I looked closely at Slinger's hands, even though they didn't look arthritic that proved nothing. Maybe he only knit rarely and didn't care which needles he used. Maybe he was just odd, I laughed. I was obsessing over trivia. Perhaps I was looking at it from the wrong angle. Since the project was on

the plastic needle it was likely that he was knitting with the plastic pair. So how did one of the plastic needles get back in his bag and a metal one end up in his neck. Did the killer extract the metal one from the yarn bag? But what were the odds of the killer grabbing that one specific needle from the bag, the only metal one in the same size? And why put the plastic one back in the bag? From the list of Slinger's needles there was a mixture of metal and plastic in different sizes but only one set of metal #6. The odds of it being a lucky grab were pretty high. How else could the killer have laid his hands on that specific needle? Could Slinger have given it to him? But why? Did Frank say, "Here, isn't this just a dandy lethal weapon?" to his glove wearing killer. I gave up and moved onto the next question.

Question: Why was the knitting upside down on his lap?
Maybe I was trying to answer a question that wasn't a question at all. Frank could have sat down and pulled his knitting into his lap and it just happened to be upside down. The only reason it might be significant is if it was the killer who put it onto Frank's lap and then only if it were for a specific purpose. So why would the killer handle the unfinished dishcloth? I was busily drawing question marks when I laughed, obviously it was because he saw a dropped stitch and wanted to correct it!

I threw down the paper in disgust. Since Tessa was unavailable I thought wine might help. The thought cheered me up. I opened a bottle of a serious red, a big burgundy and poured an indecent amount into a large glass.

Ready to tackle the unsolvable I turned back to the photo. I checked the stitches still on the needle. They weren't twisted but that only proved that anyone but Tessa could have frogged the project. Great, I laughed, I could eliminate Tessa as a suspect. On the other hand only a knitter could have left the work as it was. That meant either Slinger or the killer.

Since that made me think of Minnie I quickly moved to the next question.

Question: If Slinger was already dead how did the blood get under the unravelled yarn? And how did the pile end up so neatly arranged? This was the most perplexing of all because it had to be significant. Jack said the police thought Slinger or his killer kicked it. But that was just silly, the yarn on top was in a perfect swirl. Unless the killer was a pirouetting ballerina there had to be another explanation.

Frustrated I laid the paper aside. I needed more data. Then it occurred to me, I had more information! I jumped up, grabbed my coat and ran to the car in my slippers.

The other two boxes I'd gotten from the church were still in the trunk. How could I have forgotten? And how was I going to tell Jack about them? My only excuse was how upset I was after the break-in but that was pretty lame. Was my credibility as an expert witness blown?

Telling myself I was not procrastinating I decided to use what remained of the evening to have a quick look through the boxes. It wouldn't make any difference whether I told the police tonight or in the morning, right? And maybe I could find a vital fact, thereby redeeming myself.

Labeled, Financials, the first box was full of maintenance and repair bills for the church, mainly invoices for tuck pointing and lawn services. The only interesting, though gross document was a large bill for pest control with a note attached, "Traps cheaper, who can I get to empty them?" I could barely balance my checking account. If the solution to the murder was based on financial records then it would definitely be solved by someone else.

I was delighted when I opened the school box and found records for the Hudson Avenue Grammar School, the one across the street from my house. At least this box might be of interest to me, my father went to that school. Inside was a jumble of file folders, loose photos and even old report cards. I took the box into the living room and started organizing the information by date and type. The oldest document was a photo of the school on opening day; the latest a report card from 1962. I ended up with a large stack of yearly photos showing the entire student body. It wouldn't hurt to do a little work for the historical group so decided to scan them in. While the machine hummed I studied the photos. I didn't know the exact years my father attended but eventually found him amongst the mass of kids over a few years.

What if the burglar was looking for one of these boxes. That might explain the frustration shown by the torn booklets from the Swann Court box. But if one of these other boxes was the target then why hadn't the burglar returned for a second try? A scary thought. I reassured myself, by now the thief must think he had missed then during the break-in and that the police now had them.

Could Slinger have found something in one of these boxes to use as blackmail? No, that wasn't right, Slinger never saw these boxes, Jane told me she had just found them. That left me with the conviction that one of the boxes contained something that someone wanted bad enough to break into my house.

After I finished the photos I opened a cloud account and uploaded the images thinking it might also prove helpful to the police. When I finished I was drained. I crawled into bed and slept, dreaming of small boys and girls standing on the school's front steps their faces flickering like an old newsreel through my brain.

I woke up very early after a restless night. I had seen something while I worked and that became the basis of my dream. What was it? I made myself a coffee taking the original of the photos to the sunny kitchen table and looking at each one carefully.

The photos were labeled only with the year. There was one from 1929, the year the new school was built , a few from the 30's then almost every year to the 60's.

Three cups of coffee, a smoothie and after unearthing a magnifying glass I found it. 1968 wasn't different from any of the others except that I recognized two of the boys in the front row, Bob the handyman and standing next to him was Frank Slinger. They must be about 10 and 11 years old and the family likeness was unmistakeable. They had the same thick eyebrows in a solid line across large foreheads and they even stood the same, hunched shoulders with their feet turned out at the same odd angle. They were related.

Jack was out when I called. I left a message with his assistant about the boxes. It was a relief to have missed speaking to Jack, at least I didn't have to tell him I was an idiot for forgetting about them. Someone else would do it for me.

I went back to Ben and his burnt umber eyes. Tessa finally returned my call in the afternoon.

"I can do dinner, Thai?" she said.

"Sounds great. I'll call for a reservation, I want a booth."

"I'll meet you there, I have to get some steel wool for the Belinda's veil. "

I choked on my coffee, laughing. "I can't wait to hear," I said and rang off.

I went downstairs to get my laundry. I checked the towel in the pail. The water was now pale pink and the stain was still there. It was one of my favorite towels and I hated to turn it into a paint rag before its time. I stared at it trying to remember how it could have become soiled. I remembered bringing it downstairs with me on knit night. In my mind I retraced my steps, dropping the towel on my laundry as I went for the strawberry jam. I didn't notice the stain then and it couldn't be jam, the jar wasn't open until I was back upstairs. Then I remembered Tom Smooch following me into the basement and jumping onto the laundry pile for a nap, right on top of my towel. It hit me. This was my fleeting memory from the night of the murder. I must have seen the stain, even as the cat put it there. It had to be Frank Slinger's blood and the cat brought it from his house to mine. OMG! By soaking the towel I had innocently destroyed evidence. Not knowing quite what to do to preserve any remaining evidence and not wanting to touch it I put a lid on the pail. I was not looking forward to explaining this to Jack. I carried the pail upstairs and put it in the hall next to the boxes.

I finally had the answer to one of the knitting questions. The cat's interference with the wool explained why the pile of yarn at Slinger's feet looked odd. I pulled out the photo to see if my theory held up. The more I looked the more I was sure that it was Tom who re-arranged the pile, swirling and plumping it to make a bed in the soft cotton. While he did that he must have gotten some blood on his fur and it ended up in my basement where he made a new bed on my laundry pile depositing some, still wet, blood on my favorite towel.

It wasn't evidence that would expose the murderer but it did solve one of the puzzles from the crime scene. I felt vindicated as an expert witness and relieved that I really had seen something of significance on the night of the murder. I was deciding whether to call Jack about this new development when the doorbell rang. Constable Bradley was at the front door. I was actually glad to see him. He could deal with the pail.

I pointed to the boxes stacked neatly at the front door. "I looked through them and saw a class photo of Frank Slinger and Bob Strauss from the church. Are they related?"

"Yeah, 1/2 brothers."

I smiled, "And did you hear that I saw Carl Reid and Fred Birch arguing? Did you find out what it was about?"

"I heard it was something to do with mail. " He clamped his lips in a tight line realizing he might have said too much. Grabbing the boxes he turned to take them to the squad car sitting at the curb.

"There's something more for you to take in." When he returned I handed over the pail telling him my theory.

"You're saying that a cat with some blood on his fur walked all the way from Slinger's house to your basement?"

I nodded.

"Through the slush?"

"It isn't very much blood!" I said defensively.

"You don't know any other way Frank Slinger's blood, if it is his blood, could have gotten on a towel in your house?"

Said like that it sounded like I was his new no. 1 suspect. "No, I don't!"

He shook his head in disbelief. "We'll be in touch," he said and left, pulling out his phone as he thumped down my steps.

CHAPTER 22

When I arrived at the restaurant Tessa was already drinking tea and sketching on a serviette. Upside down it looked like a swing set and slide. I couldn't begin to think what it might be.

"I give up, what is it? A coat? Hat? Car cover?"

Tessa laughed, "Actually it's a swing set I saw at the hardware store. I'm just doodling. I was thinking of getting one for my niece."

Of course. "Let's order, I'm starved." I remembered Belinda, "What is the steel wool for?"

"Something new, old, borrowed, blue and something for the kitchen. Isn't that how the rhyme goes?"

"No. Don't tell me you are planning to knit steel wool?"

She grinned, "It's an idea but no, at least not on this project. It's to rough up the linen yarn. I want the veil to be fluffy, like a cloud around her head."

"Wow, it sounds lovely." I said sincerely. Our food arrived and we settled down to eat. It's hard to concentrate when you are chasing pad thai noodles around your bowl with chopsticks.

Once the plates were cleared I got down to business. "I may be the new no. 1 suspect in the murder of Frank Slinger," I said and told her about the boxes and the blood.

She didn't look at all concerned and said with a wink, "What does your Jack think?"

"He's not my Jack, if anyone's he's Claire's Jack." I told her what Claire had said.

She shook her head sadly, "It's what I keep saying, the good ones are always gone."

"Yeah, well, it was never anything anyway so no harm done," I said almost truthfully. "What is more important is that, as you know I've been interested in the murder and it's not just because it happened in the neighborhood. I'm doing this for Minnie's sake." And I told her about Minnie and the blackmail.

Tessa's reaction was as I guessed, "It's a given," she said firmly. "Even though Minnie looks like she did it, you and I know she couldn't have. Are you going to tell her you've told me the story?"

"Yes, eventually but I had to talk with you, I really need your advice." Telling the whole story helped make it clear. The only details I didn't share were those Jack told me in confidence, the crime scene photos and forensics. That would be breaking a promise to the police, a concept I couldn't come to terms with as easily as my duplicity with Minnie.

"We agree that the police don't know Minnie as well as we do and to them her story would make her a prime suspect.'

"So where do I go from here?" I asked.

"We, you mean. I'm in this as well!" Tessa sat back staring into space and then spoke quietly, "I think you are on the right track about the blackmail. We need to weed out the guilty from the innocent."

"That is exactly what I have been trying to do! "

"We need someone to point the police at, preferably guilty...." She said meditatively, "How about Rose?"

"Rose? Your cleaning lady? Tessa, really! What possible connection has she with Slinger?"

"She cleaned for him."

"TESSA!" I cried, "You never thought to tell me this incredibly vital piece of information?"

"I only just found out yesterday when she came to work for me. And anyway I can't imagine Rose doing anything worse than making a hole in the carpet from over-scrubbing."

"That sounds just like Camellia!" I told her about the terrible tea and bleached cookies.

"Do you think Camellia catered the memorial service for Slinger?" she giggled.

"That would make perfect sense!" I laughed.

"Anyway, back to business. Really, what about Rose? She knew Slinger and disliked him. She also knows Camellia and Oscar well. Maybe she is more involved that you think."

"Does she knit?" I asked.

"No. In fact I know she doesn't. She seems to have a thing about knitting, she won't even clean my study area. Why do you ask?"

"I was thinking of a way to talk with her."

"Why not call her and get a cleaning quote on your house?"

"Perfect! Give me her number and I'll call her in the morning. I would love to be able to have some news for Minnie at knitting. Meanwhile, can you call Claire? See if you can get her to ask Jack some questions."

"I can do that, what do we want to know?"

"Who stands to inherit? What about alibis? How about the neighbors, any feuds? Like Fred Birch and Carl Reid. Their argument was about mail apparently but in what way and is it related to the murder. Frankly I'd be happy with anything she can find out!"

I felt so much better after talking things through with Tessa that I slept soundly. On the theory that cleaning ladies get up early I called Rose while I sipped my morning coffee and fed Tom.

"Good Morning, My name is Amy Stevens. I'm friend of Tessa O'Grady and she recommended you. Do you think you could give me a quote for cleaning my house."

There was a long pause. "I don't know."

She was not very encouraging, "Tessa says you do a great job and my house is really quite small."

"I'd have to see it."

"Actually I'm home now, why don't you drop over?"

"Now?" she said, startled.

"Sure, the coffee's on!" I gave her my address then I ran around like a madwoman cleaning up for the cleaning lady.

A short time later there was a tentative knock at the door. Rose stood stiffly on the porch in the same coat and boots as at the memorial service. She was grim but not angry today.

"Please come in, This is it!" I pointed to the living room.

what does that mean?

She slipped off her boots but shrugged me away when I tried to help her with her coat.

"I'll just have a look then be on my way," she said grumpily.

"Let's go to the kitchen."

She followed me down the hall, looking right and left as she went, pausing at my studio.

"Oh, you won't be cleaning that room, it's my office." I said. "I work from home."

In the kitchen I grabbed the french press, "Coffee?" I asked, "I'm having one myself."

yes OR NO

She shook her head and sat on the edge of the pew, hunched like a large brown beetle. Without her air of fury I felt sorry for her. Trying to put her at ease I said, "Rose. That's a lovely name."

"We were named after flowers my sister and me, Rose and Camellia, " she replied stiffly.

It couldn't be! "Not Camellia Richter?"

Rose sat forward, suddenly alert and aggressive, "You know her?"

"We only just met." I said quickly, "About the historical work she and her husband do. My grandparents were early settlers."

Rose visibly relaxed.

I thought back to the argument I witnessed on the street outside the church between her, Camellia and Oscar. Sisters, another connection. So the argument was less likely to be about the murder, probably a family quarrel.

In the silence Rose was fidgeting with the strap of her bag, looking ready to bolt. "By the way, I saw you at Frank Slinger's service. Did you know him well?"

She jerked as though I had struck her, looking horrified. Standing she blurted, "I can't clean for you, I have too much to do. I have to go."

I'd touched a raw nerve. Following her down the hall I apologized, "I'm really sorry, I didn't know he meant that much to you."

She shoved her feet into her boots and her fists into her pockets, "Frank Slinger was no good to anyone I don't care about him at all."

"I heard he was such a good person, I mean he knit for the poor."

She was seething, "He was sly. Maybe he did, maybe he didn't. Whatever he did it was for his own good. You can be sure of that!"

"And his work on the historical committee? Camellia said he did things there."

"You leave my sister out of this," Rose shouted and jerked the door handle, rushing out the door.

I stared at her receding back. Rose was so wound up she could have spun the earth. Talking to her was like touching a live wire. Obviously she hated Slinger. And she was definitely protecting Camellia. But from what? From Oscar? From Slinger? From blackmail? If it was Slinger then his being dead wasn't abating her anger. I went over our conversation and couldn't come up with any clues except that she was particularly rude when I talked about Slinger's knitting for the poor.

More information but still no answers. Sherlock had Lestrade and Watson, Poirot , his Japp even Ms. Marple had Sir Henry. I had Tessa. I drummed my fingers waiting for her to get back to me. Jack hadn't called in days and Bradley probably still thought I was a suspect. Tessa was bound to call soon. Maybe Claire would know more. Otherwise I would see both of them later at knit night.

Meanwhile I thought about Rose. Did she react to my comment about Slinger's volunteering for a specific reason? If that was true then obviously I was missing something. Who could tell me more about his charity work? The Reverend Jane? No time like the present. I jumped in my car and went directly to the church.

There was no one about. Even Bob seemed to be missing which was a blessing. I wandered around to the back and knocked. It seemed awfully quiet. I waited then knocked again wondering what a Reverend might do on a Wednesday afternoon?
Returning to my car I heard a cheery 'hello' from the shrubbery. I smiled, the Reverend Harper gardens on Wednesday afternoons.

CHAPTER 23

Following the sound, I found Jane up to her ears in chickweed. She was kneeling next to a flower bed, weeding. She welcomed me with a grin and brushed a lock of hair off her face leaving a brown smudge.

"Hi, Amy!"

"Don't let me stop you. I can see you are on a mission," I grinned.

"These weeds are so persistent, they grow even in winter. I think of them as the sinners of the plant world."

I laughed. She had a wonderful sense of the ridiculous.

She sat back on her heels, "So what brings you here?"

"I was just wondering about knitting for charity. You mentioned that Mr. Slinger did that. I wonder if you could tell me more. My knitting group might be able to help."

"I'll carry on if you don't mind, I need to get this patch done so I can plant some primulas." She grabbed a big clump of weeds, "I may have exaggerated a bit. Frank Slinger did make dishcloths for a homeless group and I know they were really grateful though he didn't make very many."

"Maybe they didn't need a lot. I mean, not to sound rude but how many dishcloths does a homeless person need?"

"Not for the people!" she laughed. "They sell them in their thrift shop. It's a popular item so they always want more but Frank was only able to give them one or two a month."

"That's strange, any decent knitter can easily make one in an evening."

She stopped, looking thoughtfully at her gloves saying, "I did wonder if he might be one of those people who do things just for the effect."

"You mean to be able to say, I knit for charity, and let everyone think it's a really valuable contribution?"

"I try not to speak ill of the dead but, yes, that is exactly what I thought."

"If it makes you feel any better from what I hear about Frank Slinger you may be absolutely right."

"There is good in everyone. Maybe he had other reasons, reasons we can't imagine."

I was more skeptical, "Possibly. Did you know Bob and Frank Slinger were related?"

She went back to her weeding and answered absentmindedly, "Yes, half brothers. Bob was the one who set up the service for Frank. I must admit I was a little surprised when he asked, I mean, I knew they were related but I never saw them do more than nod at one another." She paused, "Maybe they reconciled. Recently Bob had started doing yard work at Frank's. I know because Bob asked to borrow the church's leaf blower."

She was giving me a lot to think about. "One more thing, those boxes you gave me. Did anyone else know about them? Did Bob? Or Rose, your cleaner?"

"They were in the office for a few days before you came over. Anyone could have seen them. It's unlocked as you know. Why do you ask?"

"It's nothing really but my house was broken into the other night and I have no idea what the thief was looking for. I just wondered if it could be because of the boxes."

She shook her head, "I can't imagine the dusty contents of a few old boxes would cause a burglary." She sat back and looked at me with concern, "That must have shaken you up."

"It did for a bit but then I found nothing was taken, that's why I thought it might be the boxes. Here's another long shot, do you remember which of the three boxes was the one you found in the corner?"

She looked mystified, "How can that matter?"

"If it was the boxes then knowing which one was singled out and put aside by someone other than yourself could narrow down which box was of interest to my thief. I had the idea that if someone saw them in the church and then moved it to examine or maybe to take away, perhaps that could have been the one my burglar wanted."

"I see. No, I didn't pay any attention. And why would they remove the box immediately, why just leave it?" She was a smart woman, I could see she was thinking about the ramifications of my questions.

"I don't know. As I said it was a long shot." I said with a smile, "Well it was nice chatting with you. If you think of anything, give me a call and I'll ask my knitting friends whether they'd like to make some dish cloths. Maybe that could be a good first project for you too."

She nodded, "Sounds good. See you Sunday?"

I nodded tentatively and walked around the church back towards my car. Anyone could have seen the boxes in the church. Bob, Oscar, Camellia and Rose were in and out of the church regularly. Of course, I'd told Oscar about the Swann Court box. Could he be my burglar?

Deep in thought, I unlocked the car and got in. When I reached to close my door, it was jerked out of my hand. Bob thrust his face close to mine hissing, "What do you want? Always nosing round, asking questions. I heard you taking to Jane."

I was too stunned to reply.

"If you don't leave me alone, you'll be sorry!" he said and slammed the door.

Automatically I reached up to lock the car and then sat shaking in my seat. Suddenly there was a knock on my window and I gasped. Through the distorted pane I saw Jack.

Huh?

Slowly I wound down the window.

"What's the matter?"

"Bob. He was here and he threatened me. He was really menacing and I don't know why."

"Tell me exactly what he said."

I opened the door and swung my legs around. Jack leaned against the door. I took a deep breath and staring at the ground relayed the conversation. In the repeating I could find nothing that might explain Bob's bizarre behavior. After telling Jack I felt better, "I'm not really scared but he looks so much like a deranged weasel! You turned up at the right time though, thanks. Uh, what are you doing here?"

"I have a question for the Reverend. Now I'll have a word with Bob at the same time. Since you're here, I was planning on getting back to you about the boxes and stuff. How about a quick coffee? I could meet you at Beansters in say, ten minutes."

I checked the time, nodding. I still had plenty of time before knit night so I drove straight to the coffee shop and snagged the fireplace seat. I got a latte and was relaxing in the warm atmosphere when Jack arrived and ordered a coffee and donut.

I raised my eyebrows at the donut.

"I know, a cliché, But they don't have scones." There was a pause as we sipped and he dunked.

"I'm sorry about the other boxes." I blurted, "After the burglary I completely forgot about them being in my trunk. I really was only thinking of my paintings." I didn't mention the towel.

"No problem. Our team didn't find anything useful in the Swann box and they are sure nothing is missing so that's a dead end. But whoever broke in could have been looking for something in one of the other boxes. We looked quickly through them but didn't see anything significant. It will take some time to go through them thoroughly. Who knew you had the boxes?"

"I just asked Jane Harper the same question. She said anyone could have seen them. And later I told Oscar Richter I had one."

"Which one?"

"The Swann one. He sounded very angry when I told him. But that may be because he said they contain private information for members of the historical society only."

"What about Bob?"

"Jane said that the boxes sat in the office for a while and Bob was around so yes he could have seen them. For that matter, anyone could. And anyone could have known that I took them. We made no secret of it. We can discount Jane, can't we? I mean, she gave them to me in the first place."

"Probably." He paused, "Have you considered that the burglar might have been looking for one of the boxes that was in your trunk?"

"I did, but I stopped worrying when I realized they know I would turn everything over to the police after the burglary."

"Good thing you did, eventually," he grinned.

"There was one more odd thing you should know. Jane said she put all three boxes together in the church office. When I got there two boxes were stacked next to the door and the third was on a chair in the opposite corner. Jane remarked on it, something like how did that get there? I didn't think anything about it at the time. Now I wonder if whoever saw the boxes at the church put that box aside because it was somehow important."

"Which box was it?"

"I don't know, it's so frustrating. I wasn't really paying attention and when I asked Jane she couldn't remember either."

"It may not matter," he said. "As to your burglar I think we can rule out Oscar Richter. He knew you had the Swann box and you promised to drop it off, so why would he burglarize your house?"

"True." I was reluctant to give up on Oscar as a suspect. "You did say the search was frantic and he certainly sounded upset when I talked to him. Personally I think he is just stupid enough to have done it anyway."

Jack looked skeptical. "Anything else?"

"What about the argument I saw between Carl and Fred? Was that anything to do with Slinger?"

"They both said it was over a mis-directed letter."

"That's ridiculous! It was much more heated and prolonged than that. "

"We are pursuing it. Now it's my turn, is there anything else you have forgotten to tell me?"

I blushed, "I did have a look through the other boxes before they were picked up."

He raised his eyebrows as I continued, "The only thing I came up with was that Frank and Bob are related. I understand you already knew that."

He nodded, "How did you figure it out?"

"I found a class photo of them in the school records, the family likeness was very strong when they were younger. Could Bob be the thief and hope to cover up the fact that they were related?"

"Seems unlikely as we already knew of the connection."

"Unless he didn't want it to become common knowledge. I know, that sounds lame." I hesitated, "Whoever it was, why did they rip the booklets?"

"Frustration, I guess. Hopefully we'll find a clue in one of the other two boxes."

"When can I get the Swann box back? I'd like to hand it over to the historical group."

"I can only give you photocopies. We'll have to keep the originals for a while. I'll have someone drop off the copies later today or in the morning." Another sip of coffee, "You said Bob thinks you are asking a lot of questions. Are you?"

I stammered, embarrassed, "Not really, I'm just curious and I am involved." *dont cap first 3 words*

"Have you found out anything?"

"Everything I know you probably already know or isn't important."

"Try me."

"Well Slinger was supposed to be a nice guy, I mean he knit for charity. That was a sham. I found out that his knitting contribution was so small as to be absurd. He must have wanted people to think he was a great guy."

"See," he grinned, "I didn't know that."

"So? It's not important," I said sheepishly.

"Anything else?" *half*

"Well Bob and Frank were ½ brothers and yet they didn't get along. "

"Yeah we knew that and yesterday Bob came in and confessed to finding Frank's body and making the anonymous phone call."

"Not to the killing?"

"No and before you ask he has an alibi for the actual time of the murder. "

"How good?"

"Very good. Relax, we are triple checking," he said with a raised eyebrow.

"If it's so good why did he make the phone call anonymous?"

Jack shrugged his shoulders in reply.

I continued, "And if they never had anything to do with one another what was Bob doing at Frank's?"

"Nothing sinister. It seems that their father left them a patent right in his will and from time to time they have to sign papers. This was one of those times."

"That reminds me, did Frank have a will and if so who benefits?"

"We haven't found one yet but Bob is the next of kin."

"So it's probably Bob who benefits most from Frank's death."

"Yes but," he raised his hand to stop my rebuttal, "give it up! It still won't break his alibi."

I muttered, "Maybe you aren't trying hard enough."

"I heard that," he laughed, then became serious, "tell me about the towel?"

I blushed, "I was hoping you would forget about that."

"Not a chance. We won't know if the blood is Slinger's for a while but your explanation sounds almost reasonable."

"Constable Bradley didn't think so!"

"You have to admit that it is pretty fantastic to think that the cat carried the blood through the snow to your house."

"The truth is sometimes bizarre."

"Yeah, that's why I think your story is true. Any luck on your other knit related clues?"

"No but I'm still working on them. I hope to have something soon." I said, crossing my fingers and hoping that my friends at knit night would help.

We both sat thinking for a few minutes. He seemed to be trying to decide whether to say something. So far he'd given me a lot of new information. Patiently I watched the fireplace, waiting. *what does this mean?*

He set his cup down with a thump sending the coffee into a mini tidal wave, "Have you heard anything about blackmail?"

I didn't have to fake my surprise. "Blackmail!" I repeated giving myself time to think. Since the only person I was sure was being blackmailed was Minnie and I couldn't very well tell him about her, I avoided the question murmuring, "That's terrible."

"Bob told us that Frank had something on him." He said watching me closely. His phone rang, giving me time to compose myself. He glanced at the screen, "I'll have to go," he said, "if you hear anything let me know, especially about the blackmail angle." He grabbed his jacket and left. I watched as he swung out the door. Cowboy boots. How had I missed his cowboy boots until now? Did Claire feel the same way about shoes as he and I did? I sighed.

Settling back in the chair, I sipped. Blackmail, I was glad it was out in the open and that the police were pursuing the possibility. Minnie's involvement was still my main concern. I smiled, the trail to Minnie was lined with frozen dinners but even a cowboy might have trouble following that clue.

Nevertheless I needed to warn Minnie. I called and told her it was time to tell our friends the story. We needed their help and tonight's knit night was the perfect opportunity. She finally agreed.

"Then I need to tell the Inspector too."

"Okay but wait till after we hear what the group has to say," she pleaded.

CHAPTER 24

Tonight's knit night was at Tessa's, While Tessa always provides plenty of entertainment her snacks are liable to be soda crackers and a jar of peanut butter. Therefore I was glad to see Minnie carrying a covered plate when I followed her and Mariko up the stairs. I came directly from the coffee shop with only a quick stop at home to pick up my knitting. Since my only dinner so far was the coffee sloshing in my empty stomach, even crackers sounded good.

"Minnie, don't worry. I'll do all the talking," I reassured her softly as we took off our jackets.

"Thank you, Amy," she replied.

Tessa waved from across the room, "Make yourselves comfortable!"

I love Tessa's house even though I couldn't live in it. It is a full sized shoebox diorama. Light and airy, it is monochromatic in dozens of shades ranging from cream to taupe. A floating fireplace is built into a long curved glass wall separating the living area from the bed and bathroom. Across from the fireplace on the outside wall stands a huge antique armoire, Tessa's office and showroom. When the double doors open a drawing table slides out revealing rows of cubby holes stuffed with wool samples. Notes, drawings and photos fill two full length cork boards. One note, curling and yellow around the edges read 'call Jeff!' her date from the other night must already be passe, I guessed. On the other board was a photo torn from a magazine showing a penguin lounging on an ice floe. Nearby, a scared looking model was wearing one of Tessa's knitted wrap coats. Swinging out from the top are two rods that hold Tessa's current projects. Tonight there was a vintage though still beautiful Burberry trench coat. The other had what looked like a knitted snake skin on a hanger.

"What's the Burberry for?" Jen asked.

"I'm not sure," Tessa said vaguely. "I just like it."

"And the snake?" I asked.

"What snake?"

"That," I pointed.

"That is a ruffle I am making for a purse," she held up a plain black bag.

I looked back at the skin imagining the ruffle. "Who is it for?"

"Hermies. It's a one off for a photo shoot," she said pushing magazines and papers off the coffee table.

"You don't mean Hermes?" I asked, giving the designer it's French pronunciation.

She nodded looking secretly pleased.

"You are moving up in the world!" I congratulated her.

At the far end of the room, in the kitchen area, Minnie and Mariko were setting out their goodies while Jen put an off-white kettle on the cream stove.

"Where's George?" I called.

Jen answered, "Tim and Ross played hooky and went fishing this afternoon. They weren't home when I was ready to go so George said she'd take the kids and wait for them. She said she was tired anyway and she might not make it."

"And Claire must have other plans, she sent a text a while ago, " Tessa added.

With Jack? Perhaps that was who phoned him at the coffee shop. Stop it! I told myself.

When we finally settled down, I began, "I need your help, all of you, so I want you to listen to a story." It took a while to tell what I knew. Even though Tessa and Minnie knew different parts of the story I wanted to repeat it all to get the information straight in my mind.

When I was finished I looked around. Minnie was relaxed, looking relieved. Tessa was thoughtfully chewing the rubber tip of her needle protector.

"So now you know as much as I do." I turned to Tessa, "What did Claire tell you?"

She looked mystified.

"About what the Police know but aren't telling the newspapers?" I prompted.

"Sorry, I forgot to call her. I'll do it first thing in the morning."

"Actually I don't think you need to. I saw Jack today and he told me a lot," I said. "The important thing is that the police know Frank was a blackmailer. And they think that is the motive."

Jen spoke first. "And you want to help them find someone who hasn't got an alibi and was being blackmailed and you've narrowed it down to Rose, Camellia and Oscar, Carl and Fred, right?"

I nodded. "Yes. Starting with the alibis, only Bob's is airtight. From what Jack said the rest are unsubstantiated, including

Minnie 15 unfortunately.   And from what I've found out, all of them are probable blackmail victims."

"Good," Tessa smiled, "now what?"

There was a pause before Jen suggested, "How about we try this?" She reached down and pulled a pad of sticky notes out of her knitting bag. "Clear the table please."

I laughed. "Perfect.   We'll finally see Jen's Sticky System in action!"

"Look and learn," she grinned as she wrote a different note for each of the following, sticking them in a line on Tessa's glass coffee table top.
Rose
Camellia
Oscar
Bob
Carl
Fred

"I'm including Bob for the moment.   Let's think of all the connections between any of these people and Slinger.   Just call them out and I'll write"

Post Office
Historical society
Church
Cat
Car
1/2 brothers HALF
Neighbour feuds

"Sisters," Tessa called out.

Jen stopped, "What has that got to do with Slinger?"

"Maybe nothing but I thought you meant we should say anything that any of the people had in common with each other not just with Frank."

"Right. That makes sense" I agreed. "Add Reverend Harper though not as a suspect," I laughed, "but as a common thread. By the way she wants to learn to knit! After this is all over I'll invite her to one of our evenings. I thought she might start on dishcloths for the homeless thrift shop."

"Wonderful idea," said Jen. "Okay, back to business,

"Knitting for charity," Minnie said.

"And computer skills," Jen added.

There was a lull, "Is that it?" Jen asked. We nodded. "Ok so let's change tack and list how each of our suspects was making their blackmail payments."

I watched her place 'house cleaning' over Rose's name and 'yard work' over Bob's. No one mentioned Minnie's frozen dinners.

"What could Oscar and Camellia have paid with?" she asked.

"Maybe all Oscar had to do was support Frank in the historical committee meetings, though that seems a little lame." Tessa said.

"True," but she wrote 'agreement' on a note.

"What about if Oscar was being pressured to give Frank historical documents, the kind from which he could find all sorts of new blackmail victims?" Tessa mused.

"That sounds better!" Jen wrote 'documents/new targets' and placed it on Oscar. "How about Camellia? What could she have done for him?"

"Clean the car?" Mariko said.

"You mean the '57 in the garage?" I asked.

Mariko nodded.

"You could be right. It is kept in immaculate condition and Camellia is certainly a thorough cleaner like her sister Rose. Perhaps she and Rose did it in payment. "

Jen placed the car sticky between Camellia and Rose.

I looked at the stickies, "Ok, Carl and Fred were arguing about something. What if they are accomplices in a blackmail scheme and were having a falling out?"

"That would explain the argument," Tessa agreed.

Suddenly the sticky note system made sense. The list of victims and their possible penalty payments were clear and we had a long list of common factors that linked one or more people to Slinger. Visually it was easier to make the connections.

"It would also explain the possible tie-in to the post office. I mean if Slinger was using confidential information from the post office as another source of blackmail material then since he retired he'd need an inside guy and that could be Fred. I'm not sure how to fit Carl into things except that as a nosey neighbor he might have guessed what was going on and so became part of the scheme. The murder could be as simple as a power struggle, " I said reflectively.

"True, but let's do a bit more brainstorming, " Jen encouraged.

"You're right, it's easy to get sidetracked. Let's start with Bob. The only factor I know that connects him to Slinger is the fact that they are 1/2 brothers. And remember even if Bob was being blackmailed he can't be the murderer, at least not directly. "   HALF

"But this whole exercise is to find blackmail victims and connections, not necessarily the murderer. That comes later," Tessa replied.

Jen stuck 'half brothers' over Bob. "Ok, back to connections. What about Oscar?"

"The historical society, for sure," Tessa declared.

"And Camellia?"

"I think she is more scared of her husband than she was of Slinger," I said.

Mariko said softly, "Maybe she is only shy."

Minnie finally spoke. "Perhaps, but it sounds more like she simply doesn't know anything. Could Camellia be paying for something Oscar did, not realizing it is a blackmail payment?"

"Sure, makes sense" I agreed.

Jen placed Camellia next to Oscar.

"And Rose? Other than the fact that she is Camellia's sister I don't   think any of the other slips apply." Jen said thoughtfully.

"The sisters could share a secret," Minnie said.

"True. But what kind of secret could they share that could cause them to be blackmailed?"

"They're illegitimate!" Tessa cried.

"Nobody cares about that anymore," Jen sniffed.

"Some people do. Though I agree that Rose seems too hard boiled to care about what side of the blanket she came from. She could be protecting her sister, I guess. What next?" I asked, watching Jen use the Sisters note to connect Rose and Camellia.

"Now let's see if we can narrow down the factors so we know where to focus our energy," Jen said methodically. "Post office. Minnie, do you know anything about his old postal route?"

She hesitated, "I think he only worked in the office I don't think he actually ever delivered mail."

"Do we know anyone in the post office?" Tessa asked the group. "Is there a way to prove our theory that Carl and Fred were Slinger's accomplices?"

There was a long pause while Jen placed the post office note between the two names.

I was remembering the look Carl gave me and how unsettled it made me feel. "Maybe we should leave them to the police."

Jen nodded tapping the table, "Okay, Church. Did Frank go to the church?"

Minnie nodded, "Sometimes."

"Maybe that's the blackmail connection to Bob. Maybe Bob did something at the church and Frank saw," Tessa said.

It was a new thought, "Good idea, but what? Remember his only punishment seems to be Frank's lawn work so whatever Bob did it can't be very bad."

"Maybe he falsified some bills for maintenance? Something that was in that Financial box," Tessa suggested.

"It might make sense that it is something to do with the church finances but Slinger never knew about the Financial box, it was discovered after he died. Of course he could have found out some other way, some other records, I haven't been able to find out what Slinger was working on before he died. I tried asking Camellia but she said I'd have to ask Oscar"

Mariko asked innocently "Did you?"

"You don't know how scary he is, I've put it on hold," I confessed.

"I'll ask him," Tessa said looking me squarely in the eye.

"Not without protection," I promised. Looking at the stickies I asked, "How about Tom Smooch, the Cat? " My question was met with blank stares. I smiled, "Good! Tom doesn't deserve to be mixed in with this bad company." I said and stuck that note on my knitting bag.

"Knitting for charity?" Jen read out. "Did Rose say anything to you that could be a clue?"

"She really hated Slinger and went kind of weird and got really angry when I mentioned Frank's knitting for the poor," I said while Jen put that sticker next to Rose. "But I can't see anything in that."

"Okay, we've got Reverend Harper and computer skills left. Actually I think those are just ways Frank got information," Jen finished.

There was silence as we all studied the slips.

I picked up 'Computer skills' and put it on Oscar. "He's the only one of the four who seems to use a computer besides Slinger, not that it matters I guess."

Mariko picked up 'Rev. Harper' and placed it above and not touching all the rest.

Minnie asked, "Why there, Mariko?"

"She is Minister. She should be at top."

There was a collective smiling sigh of approval.

"Seriously Jen, this really has helped clarify things." I said sincerely. "I take back anything I ever said about you being disorganized."

"I just wish they made sticky notes that are a bit stickier" Jen laughed.

Looking back at the table, I said, "I think we should focus on Oscar. He's the most connected. What do you think?"

"I think this shows that everyone," Tessa pointed at the stickies, "is probably a blackmail victim, plus there may be a whole lot more. And any of them could have done the murder," she summed up despondently.

"Yes, but that's always been the case and while I know that most of this is supposition I feel we are getting closer. Tessa, you and I will find a way to talk to Oscar and either Claire will find out what the police know about Carl and Fred or I'll ask them myself. At least it is something concrete to do!" I looked down at the three rows of knitting I had finished in the past hour and knew I'd have to rip them back. So while the knitting was a washout I did feel like we made progress.

CHAPTER 25

BROUGHT

Constable Bradley bought a large folder with the photocopies of the Swann booklets early the next morning. I tried to sound innocent as I asked, "How is the blackmail angle working out?"

Bradley was startled, "What about blackmail? Who said anything about that?"

Maybe Jack wasn't sharing that insight and that was good news for Minnie's sake at least in the short term. I decided to plant a little seed and see if it worked it's way back to Jack. "I heard that Bob confessed to being blackmailed," not strictly the truth but close, "and I just wondered if the blackmail idea extended to Carl Reid and Fred Birch?"

"Why them?"

"Doesn't it seem logical? Slinger and Birch worked together at the post office and Reid knew them both. A lot of private information goes through the Queen's mail." I was really stretching my theory but it seemed like such a good idea the night before. Maybe I could even give Constable Bradley a career boost. "You could suggest the connection to Inspector Sommerville and see what he thinks."

Bradley nodded slowly, "Yeah, maybe."

I was pleased, one of my plans was in motion.

Tessa called to say that Claire was in Seattle and wouldn't be able to talk till the following day.

"By that time I will have read the court booklets. The police dropped off the photocopies." I replied.

"Why bother?"

"I guess because this was the information that Oscar was frantic about."

"You've already scanned them. Why haven't you looked at them before now?"

"I never thought they had anything of interest but after yesterday I figure it can't hurt. And the guy's handwriting is so bad the recognition program makes a lot of mistakes. It's actually easier to read the photocopies."

"Have fun," she said as she rang off.

I started looking through the pages looking for any names I recognized. There it was... Rose and Camellia.

The date was March 1955. The case had very few details, it didn't even fill the page. Social Services was asking for a stop in visitation rights for a father only noted as JT. It was noted that the father had numerous prior reprimands for violating the terms of contact with his two daughters, 9 and 4, now in foster care. The judge ruled that the father would still be allowed to spend time with the girls but only if supervised ~~by~~ *But* by Social Services. None of the people were named ~~by~~ Swann had written in the margin, "Rose very angry. Camellia lost."

Sisters named Rose and Camellia and about the right ages, it had to be them. Why were the girls in public care if their father was still in the picture? Why did the father have to be supervised when visiting his own daughters? Where was the mother? And finally why was 9 year old Rose angry? It was such a small note, easily missed. Could this reference be why someone broke into my house?

I quickly read through the rest of the pages and found nothing else of interest.

I thought about the new information while I spent the rest of the day re-painting Murray the flop-eared bunny for April. Murray was turning out to be the cutest rabbit ever. His long ears puddled around his paws. Using a brush with only a few hairs I painted each individual hair so that his fur looked 3D and soft enough to stroke. Painting this slowly gave me a lot of time to think.

The police must have picked up this clue. Jack mentioned a team looking at the box but were they thorough enough? Did they realize it was this box that Oscar Richter made such a fuss about?

Rose and Camellia were taken away from their parents. The father was somehow proving to be difficult. There was no mention of the mother. Was there a motive for murder buried somewhere in this for Rose, Camellia or even Oscar? There wasn't anything else in the Swann booklets about the family but maybe there would be more coverage in the local papers from around the time.

Tomorrow was the historical committee meeting in the library basement. I knew the library carried copies of old newspapers. It was kismet, a sign. I'd go to the meeting early and do a little digging through the archives.

Tessa called the next morning while I was having breakfast. "Hi, guess what I found out?"

"Good morning to you too!"

"Yeah, yeah. I finally connected with Claire," she said impatiently. "Bob was your burglar!"

"I don't know if that makes me feel better of worse!"

"Claire said Bob confessed to the police that he saw the box at the church and planned to take it but you got there first. He was so mad he broke into your house but couldn't find the right box! That's when he started ripping and throwing."

"Which box did he want?"

/ HALF

"The school one. He knew that there would be references to the fact that he and Frank were 1/2 brothers and he didn't want anyone to find out so he thought he would just steal the information."

"What difference does it make it they are brothers?"

"Did I mention that Jack thinks Bob is 5 cans short of a sixpack?"

I laughed. "Somehow I knew it must have been someone like Bob, he's more slimy than dangerous. Did he say why he destroyed my painting?"

"You're going to love this! He said that he thought it was a portrait of him and Frank and that you were mocking him!"

"For heaven's sake! It was a couple of ferrets! Oh! Do you think I was subconsciously painting his portrait?"

"Too bad he wrecked it, Bob as a ferret would be perfect!"

"When did the police find out he was the burglar?" I was a little peeved that Jack was telling his girlfriend before me, the robbery victim.

"Last night. Claire talked with Jack this morning before she called me."

I didn't want to think about where this early morning chat took place.

Tessa was bursting, "But Amy, I have more! The reason Bob was being blackmailed was their father's will."

"Claire told you that?" She must be close if Jack would tell her confidential information.

"Yes, who else?   It turns out that there was a deathbed revision to their father's will. It wasn't a big thing, something about Bob being named executor instead of Frank and getting a greater share of the total inheritance."

"That the reason for the blackmail?"

"Yup, think about it, Frank was an experienced blackmailer so it was easy for him to convince Bob that he could challenge the will. He told Bob he could prove the old man was gaga at the time of the revision and then get all the money. True or not, the important part is that Bob believed his brother. Claire said Jack told her in the matter of blackmail it often doesn't matter what the secret is, just how much the victim doesn't want it discovered."

"Makes sense. Did Bob do Frank's yard work as payback?"

"So he says."

"Was his the only evidence of blackmail that the police found?"

"Claire asked the same thing and at that point Jack acted a bit cagey. He said they were exploring other avenues. She said even though she pressed he wouldn't say anything more."

"Do you think they know about Minnie?"

"Probably not or they would have questioned her. But everyone knows that when blackmail is involved there is often more than one target. So what did you find out?"

I told her about the Tomson court case.

She voiced my suspicions, "That sounds like more blackmail material doesn't it?"

"It sure does. Anyway I plan to go to the archives and check it out on my way to the historical committee meeting."

"Do you want me to come with you to the meeting? If Oscar is there it could be a good time to confront him together."

"No, let's wait. If he's there I'll just play it by ear. I really don't think we will get anything out of him if we go head to head. And until I have exhausted all the other options I don't want to try. Anyway, right now I'm going to call Minnie and see if she is going to the meeting."

"Try to encourage her not to go, the last thing she needs is confrontation and if Oscar is there that's what she will get! What are you going to do over the weekend? We still haven't gone shopping."

"I can't even think about shopping. I have to devote myself to painting for a while or this month's bills are going to paid late!"

"I know the feeling," she said sympathetically.

When I hung up I dialled Minnie. I smiled when she picked up on the first ring and I could hear the click of her knitting needles in the background. Maybe things were back to normal.

"Amy, how nice to hear from you."

"Minnie, how are you?"

"Better. Mariko is such a nice girl. She said when her English gets good enough she is going to write a letter to the placement agency telling them what a wonderful host I am."

"That's great. "

"Have you found out anything new?" I could hear the anxiety creeping back into her voice.

"No, not really but I want to ask you something. I see that the historical society is meeting on Monday night, do you plan to go?"

"No. Besides the fact that I don't wish to see Camellia for the moment, they are planning an event that I'm not part of so I haven't gone to the last few meetings. Why do you ask? "

"Oh I just wondered.   I'm kind of interested in my Grandfather's role in the city so I thought I might check it out."

"Watch out for Julie, she'll have you licking stamps before you know it!" she laughed. And," she hesitated, "you will let me know if you hear anything?"

I assured her I would.

Over the weekend, I focused on my real job and spent it painting three turtles on a log for February. I dubbed them Larry, Curly and Moe.

On Monday Tessa rang to say that she was going to call Oscar Richter to find out what Frank was working on just before he died. "I'm tired of waiting and he can't do anything over the phone," she assured me.

"You're insane! How are you going to persuade him to tell you? He's never met you!"

"I'm going to tell him the truth, sort of, that I'm fact checking for the police."

"TESSA! You can't!"

"Why not? All I'm asking is a simple question."

I sighed. "You better use a pay phone so he doesn't have your phone number and don't tell him your name!"

Tessa didn't report back by the time I left to drive to the library. I used the hour before the meeting learning to load microfiche into an old fashioned reader. On the theory that whatever happened to the Tomson family must have happened prior to March 1955 I started then and worked my way backward. Time flew by and I was only at the beginning of 1954 when I had to shut it down to go to the meeting. I realized just how long the job could take. Was it even necessary? Could I find out another way? I could ask Jack, of course. Maybe I would.

CHAPTER 26

I made my way down to the basement meeting rooms and stood in the doorway, it was not encouraging. The room itself was small and a depressing shade of brown. There was a long table in the centre with mis-matched chairs around it. The four seniors milling about the table were at least 30 years older than me and none was familiar. It looked about as lively as a funeral. There was no sign of Oscar or Camellia.

"Helloooo," an elderly lady in horn rimmed glasses called out, "are you Amy Stevens?"

"Yes, how did you know my name? Oh right, the librarian must have told you I was coming."

She twinkled, "Yes, she's very efficient. Welcome to the historical society and we're the local dinosaurs. Come on in and I'll introduce you."

"I'm Julie." I smiled remembering Minnie's advice to avoid her. Then I was introduced to Walt, John and Beth Ann.

"There may be a few stragglers but we don't worry about them. We start on time and leave on time." Everyone smiled as they shuffled to a seat, I did too.

Walt started, "We need to finalize the Dig."

I perked up, "Dig, as in archaeological dig?"

Beth Ann giggled, "Sort of."

Walt held up a hand, "Ok, I guess we need a quick recap for the newbie. Next month we are planning a fundraising event called Dig It! The space behind city hall is going to be a new community garden so we decided to use it first. We're bringing in the rototillers a weekend early to churn up the ground and then we will plant a bunch of easy to find archeological artifacts. We're in the final planning stages. This meeting is to ensure everyone is on task."

Beth Ann spoke first; "I got a load of old tools from various garage sales, basically anything I could pick up for free. John?"

"I weeded through Beth Ann's finds and found some good stuff which I put on craigslist, so far we've made $157. The rest is good to be buried."

"Julie?"

"Our call for old china has given us so much I don't think we'll ever run out. John agreed that it was a load of rubbish so I'm having a great time smashing it." I must have looked as appalled as I felt. She grinned at me, "Actually, I'm gently breaking a few things and will stash the pieces in the dig. When they are 'found' we'll glue them together at the artifact table."

"Great, and I've been making up all kinds of fake documents on my computer. I think that's it." Walt turned to me, "Amy, have you anything to add?"

I was stunned, "This is fantastic! I can't think of anything right now but I would love to help, I've always wanted to be on a dig," I added shyly.

Walt replied, "Good. We'll need lots of volunteers." The remainder of the meeting centred on security, the 'gate', the refreshment tent and parking. It was all under control. I shook my head, a bunch of old people I'd called them. I better revise my own old fashioned ideas, I was exhausted just listening to their energetic plans.

We stopped for tea and cookies. Store bought cookies! I could fix that next time. Then Camellia came in, alone. Could the evening get any better? She sat and though no one said anything I saw John mouth 'chin up'. Beth Ann brought her a cup of tea and Walt gave her shoulder a squeeze.

"I'm sorry I'm late," Camellia said in a soft sad voice, "since I'm not really involved with the dig I didn't think it mattered."

"It doesn't. We're all finished anyway. Just enjoy your tea," Julie said.

It was interesting that the group liked Camellia. I moved to sit next to her. "I'm new here and very excited about helping with the dig," I said honestly. "What is your area of interest?"

"I just help out where I can." She looked around helplessly.

"I want to help too." I said sincerely. "I'm actually very good at organizing..." She didn't react so I said encouragingly, "you know, papers and computer work, like I said before."

"Oh. Really?"

I nodded, "You must be overwhelmed by the work that Franks' death left behind."

"I don't know what to do with all the papers," she said distressed. "This afternoon the police brought over all the papers from Frank's and it's a mess."

Bingo! This must be the last things he was working on.

"Do you know what they are?"

"Oh no!" she said shocked. "I don't even want to touch them!"

"I can imagine." I mused. "Could I help? How about I come over after the meeting and have a look?"

"I don't know. Oscar hasn't seen them yet, and he's not even home."

"It'll be fine. I'll just stop in for a second. I am sure Oscar will appreciate any help he can get. Now that I am part of the committee he can't have any objection."

It worked, she was convinced. "Okay I guess you can come over, but just for a quick look."

As the meeting wrapped up I offered to bring homemade cookies to the next meeting. Camellia and I went to our cars and I followed her as she drove home. At the house I headed straight for the boxes that were stacked in the centre of her living room. I tried not to sound as enthusiastic as I felt, "I'll just take a quick peek and be on my way."

I looked at the first box, labeled "Land Records". It was stuffed with yellowed documents. It looked like all the boxes were a mess, papers shoved in. Slinger must have been through them all but didn't bother to keep them in any order. Knowing I needed to act quickly as Oscar could come home anytime, I skimmed the titles on the boxes.

It was hard to contain my excitement when I found it, "This one, Port Oxford Gazette Court Reports 1948 to 1959 looks interesting. It's just a bunch newspaper articles. It's not even confidential." I picked up the box giving her my winningest smile.

Camellia spluttered, "Maybe…."

"Not to worry , I'll just organize it, put them in date order. That will show Mr. Richter that I can do the job." I was at the door opening it with my free hand. "I'll bring it back in a few days. Don't even tell him I have it, it'll be my surprise!" I walked quickly to my car, loaded the box in the back and drove off. That went well, I thought smugly.

It was still early when I got home so I made myself a cup of tea and opened the box. After putting them in order I started at March 1955 and worked backwards again. Even though I'd already looked at the microfiche it was possible I missed something. Soon I was immersed in the trivia of my city. I got all the way to the beginning of 1950 without finding anything. With a distinct lack of enthusiasm I went back to March 1955 and slowly worked my way forward. Finally, I found it. There were a series of articles beginning on November 12,1955 with the news of the death of Joseph Tomson, Rose and Camellia's father. Picking out the details I read that the body of Tomson was found in his kitchen. He died as a result of a knife wound to the stomach and bled to death. The only other people in the house at the time were his two daughters, who were asleep in their beds. When the girls awoke they found their father and ran outside screaming. Later articles revealed that Tomson had very high levels of alcohol in his system. It was suggested that while in a drunken state he slipped, falling on the knife he was using to make a sandwich. Eventually the case was ruled death by misadventure.

There was a separate series of articles concerning the subsequent investigation into Social Services because of the case. I learned that on the day of his death Joseph Tomson was on a supervised visit with his daughters. He, his daughters and the case worker were at a restaurant in a distant part of town. As soon as the worker went to the bathroom Tomson grabbed the girls and drove away leaving the social worker stranded at the restaurant. It turned out the social worker was so embarrassed he failed to follow procedure and so the girls were alone with their father overnight, the same night he died.

I sat back. He basically kidnapped his daughters. They must have been terrified. Then they found him dead the next morning. I couldn't image the trauma they went through. I skimmed forward and didn't see any more references to the case. So much was left out. Was it possible for two young girls to sleep through what must be a messy and noisy way to die? I didn't know much about bleeding to death. Surely it must take some time, time that he was conscious and vocal. And yet the girls slept through the whole thing. Odd and not very likely, I guessed.

It was time to call Jack. He picked up on the first ring but sounded busy so I quickly told him what I knew about the Tomson's. He promised to get back to me later.

While I waited for him to call I started on Tina the hedgehog. She was to be December and I was working from a series of photos I'd taken last Christmas when I borrowed Tina from the SPCA. She had discovered the joy of discarded bows and wrapping paper and was adorable. The time passed quickly. I was just finishing for the day when the doorbell rang.

Jack stood on the front step.

"You look exhausted," I said as I held the door open.

"It's been a hell of a day. I wanted to come by and thank you for the stuff about the Tomson case. We had some of it but with your tip we dug deeper. I think this may be the information we need to break this case."

"Off duty?" I asked.

He nodded.

"Beer?"

"I'd love one," he said simply.

I got out a couple of bottles and glasses then took out some chips and fresh salsa. We sat in the kitchen, Jack dug in with gusto. Then he chugged half the beer and visibly relaxed in the pew. "I looked up the original case files. You've got the highlights."

"Was there anything about how long it would have taken him to die and whether he was conscious?"

"Very clever," he said. I beamed.

"The knife actually entered his stomach at an upward angle and punctured his diaphragm and one lung. So he would have died within ten minutes and should have been conscious and able to call out." He held up his hand, "But before you ask, the girls were questioned by social workers, doctors and a psychiatrist. Camellia was in shock, remember she was only four and said she didn't hear anything. None of doctors felt that they got the full truth from Rose but they concluded that while she was probably hiding something it was irrelevant." He paused, "I also looked into the files on Joseph Tomson. He had a long record of violence and drunkenness. There were a bunch of complaints made by his wife, the girls' mother, for abuse, all later withdrawn. The last note on the mother was by a social worker who called at the home and found that she had moved out, leaving the kids. A short while later the father ended up overnight in jail. At that point social services stepped in and took them into care. Rose was eight at the time and Camellia three."

"I hate to say it but his death sounds awfully convenient."

"Go on."

"I'm not saying I think Rose or Camellia actually killed their father. But I do think Rose could have been hiding the fact that she heard him call out and ignored him, or she got up and went into the kitchen and saw him but waited till morning before discovering him."

"Why do you think Rose would do that?"

"What if the abuse didn't stop with the mother? What if after she left the girls became the target?"

"Could be but there is no way to prove it."

"No but could it be a basis for blackmail?"

"What makes you think Rose was being blackmailed?"

"Because she cleaned house for Slinger. Bob does his lawn, Rose his cleaning, it makes sense."

"Interesting. Any other theories?"

"Camellia and Oscar could also be targets. Camellia said Oscar recently began to agree with everything Frank wanted on the historic committee even though in private he hated him. That sounds odd, doesn't it?"

Jack didn't say anything so I continued, "Could Frank have been holding the same threat over all three of them?"

"You make some interesting points." He said as he got up. "I've got an appointment I can't break and I still have a report to write but I'll be in touch."

An appointment at this time of night? Probably with Claire. I followed him to the door.

He pulled on his coat, "Oh and I almost forgot. The blood on your towel was Slinger's and there were cat hairs mixed in so even Constable Bradley believes your story," he grinned. "I'll call tomorrow if I have anything more."

CHAPTER 27

The kitchen was empty and quiet after Jack left. Then I heard rustling on the back porch and opening the back door found Tom preparing a bed out of dead leaves.

"Come on in Tom Smooch you can be my dinner date."

I opened another beer and finished the salsa, Tom ate some leftover stir fry. I watched him delicately pick out the chicken and broccoli leaving everything else behind.

Tessa called a bit later to report that she'd had second thoughts about calling Oscar.

"Good, I can save you the trouble." I told her about finding the box of records with the court notes concerning the death of Rose and Camellia's father.

"I'm confused, didn't you already read through the court box? Is there another one?"

"Of course!" I said as the light finally dawned, "I'm such an idiot! There are two Court boxes. The one I got from the church is Joe Swann's notes and the one I got from Camellia which came originally from Frank Slinger had the Gazette newspaper court accounts." Finally the pieces were coming together. "I told Oscar I had a court box. He had no idea that I was talking about Joe Swann, he didn't even know the second box existed."

Tessa nodded, "Okay, you have the Swann box and the Gazette box, I still don't get it."

"I think Frank was using the information he learned from the Gazette Box to blackmail Oscar and now Oscar thought I had that same information. Wow, no wonder he was livid."

"Mad enough to murder?"

"Sounds like it. I need to call Jack and tell him."

I ended up calling the station. Jack's phone was off and he wasn't taking messages. He was probably having too much fun on his date, I thought sourly.

I left a detailed message with the officer on duty.

Later that night Jack called to say that he got the message and Oscar was being brought in for questioning. He said he'd try to let me know the details later.

The next day I painted then did some cleaning around the house, shaking the dust off my knitting. It was knit night at my house and I realized I hadn't done a single stitch since the last social. I made peanut butter chocolate chip cookies for the girls putting some in the freezer for the next historical meeting.

By evening I hadn't heard anything new from Jack. I took it as a good sign that he didn't have time to call. It might mean the case was solved.

Claire arrived early, "I really miss our socials but now I'm back for a whole month!"

"Yes, we have a lot of catching up to do." I smiled, she was still a good friend. It wasn't her fault I'd taken a shine to her boyfriend in her absence.

Tessa flew through the door asking Claire sweetly, "How is Jack?"

Claire, looked a little surprised, "How do you know Jack?"

"I tend to keep track of good looking men I meet," she said winking at me.

"You're right, he is good looking!" She said with a smile, deftly avoiding Tessa's question and turning to Minnie who came up the steps followed by Mariko. "Minnie, I haven't seen you in ages. How are you?" she asked.

Minnie looked happy. She was wearing a t-shirt that read "I'd rather be knitting!" in pink sequins. Jen arrived announcing that George was in Kelowna for a trial and wouldn't be coming.

I brought them up to date as we settled down to knit. We agreed, it looked like the police had the case wrapped up.

Minnie was making a fluffy blue baby bootie and looked the picture of grandmotherly love. Mariko was working on a matching set in doll size and Jen was finishing up a brown slouch hat. "My kids are either selling their hats on the black market at their elementary school or they lose them faster than I can knit new ones."

Claire's rectangular scarf in chocolate brown with flecks of red and orange was almost finished. Tessa seemed to be knitting a swirl of orange, red and black.

"What's that going to be?" I asked.

"It's a teacosy" she said whipping it upside down to show me. "I think it looks like a mini dragon," she grinned, "Get it? Firebreathing hot!" I groaned as the doorbell rang.

Jack? I hoped not, this could be awkward. I glanced at Claire but she was busy casting off.

The bell rang again, whoever was there was holding the button down. I opened the door and Rose pushed into me screaming incoherently, "You! You had to poke your nose in. You leave Camellia alone!"

Then she noticed the group. They sat with their projects in midair, mouths agape. Rose looked from one to the other as the blood drained from her face. She uttered a sob and crumpled to the ground.

I was closest but Jen was faster. She sprang to her feet and thrust a cushion under Rose's head.

"Get a cool cloth and glass of water," she commanded.

When I returned from the kitchen Jen was talking to her softly. Slowly Rose started to come around then caught sight of me and struggled to sit up. Some of her anger returning she growled, "You! You sent that cop to Camellia. You shouldn't have done that, Camellia doesn't understand."

Jen held the cup of water I'd brought, urging her to drink. Rose took a sip, the fight and anger draining away leaving her tired and deflated.

"You protect Camellia, don't you?" I said gently.

Rose stared at me, "She's my sister. I'm all she has."

"What about your parents?"

"The best thing my father ever did was die," she murmured, "and her..." she stopped, saw Minnie and went rigid, "get away from me!" she screamed.

"What? Me?" Minnie squeaked and shrank into her chair.

"You're just like my mother!" Rose spat hysterically.

"How is Minnie like your mother?" I asked bewildered.

Rose was ranting, "Mother! Don't call her that. You know what she did, all day every day? Nothing but knit. She didn't care about us. All I ever heard was them yelling or the click of her needles. Do you have any idea how much I hate that sound," Rose scrambled to her feet, "click, click, click. It never stopped." She was remembering, reliving, "Do you know what he did? Noooo ... you were too busy knitting. Well I'll tell you, I'll tell you all! After we went to bed the yelling would start. The more he drank the louder it got but when it went quiet that was worse. Then all I could hear was the click of her needles and his footsteps coming to my room. Even after that woman, she was no mother to us, left I could still hear her needles whenever..." she broke off shuddering. "Abuse. That's what social services called it," she said spitting, "such wickedness. Abuse. I warned Camellia, I told her to crawl under the bed and cover her ears so she never heard that word. "

Poor Camilla was only four when she knew the meaning of abuse. Twice in the last few of days that word had brought a look of revulsion to Camellia's face.

"You were very young," Jen said gently, helping her to a chair.

"Young? Ha! When he started looking at Camellia I knew that I would have to do something. She was only a baby! It was my job to look after her," she said fiercely.

"Yes, I understand." I said quietly, the pieces falling into place.

She relaxed a bit.

I sat on the ottoman across from her, "How did your father die?" I asked.

"I didn't kill him if that is what you mean," she sneered. "I didn't help him though. Why should I?"

"And Slinger? Did he find out?"

"He said he would tell people that Camellia killed our father. Camellia doesn't remember anything, she didn't even wake up that night. Her life would have been ruined."

"What did you do?"

"I paid. It was a nightmare. I had to clean his house. Every week he reminded me of what I went through. Every week he sat in his chair and knit. It drove me crazy. Somehow he figured out that I didn't mind plastic needles as much as the metal ones, the sound," she covered her ears, whispering, "She always knit with metal needles."

I realized she was talking about her mother again. "What happened?" I prompted.

"That night when I came in to clean he was knitting. When he saw me he stuck one of the needles in his bag and pulled out a metal one waving it in my face saying, you like the metal ones best, don't you? I wonder what more can I get you to do for me so that I stop knitting?"

"I knew what he meant. Slinger was just like my father, like all men, dirty and disgusting. I couldn't stand it, I grabbed at the needle." She looked dazed, remembering, then roused herself, "He did it himself! He tried to grab me. It wasn't my fault! The bastard did it to himself!"

In the shocked silence the doorbell rang. I got up quickly, Jack was on the porch. I slid past him, pulling the door behind me.

"What's wrong?" he asked.

"Rose is in there and she just told us how Slinger died," I whispered. He called for back up. I led him back inside. Rose had not moved and she didn't say a word as she was cautioned and taken into custody. Claire followed shortly thereafter.

Standing at the door Jen brought up George's absence. "I doubt any of this would have come out if George had been here."

I agreed, "George would not have allowed a potential client to confess. I wonder what George's colleagues will say when they find out that her cleaner is a murderer?" We both smiled as she left.

Minnie and Mariko were the last to leave. Mariko was already on the porch when Minnie turned back and said quietly, "I'll come over in the morning," before she followed Mariko down the stairs. I didn't bother to ask why and it was well after midnight when I finally tumbled into bed.

CHAPTER 28

Good as her word Minnie showed up the next morning just in time for coffee.

"You must be relieved it's all over," I said as I poured her a cup.

"Yes, but I have a confession to make. I'm really sorry but there is something I didn't tell you."

"You were there that night, in the house with Slinger, weren't you?"

"How did you guess?" Minnie asked bewildered.

"When Rose told us how Slinger died I realized I had the answer to the last of my knitting questions. She said that there was a struggle, so his knitting must have fallen to the floor." Minnie nodded as I continued, "Since it was upside down on his lap when the police showed up I asked myself who could have put it there? Rose wouldn't have touched it. She hated knitting.   I don't know when Bob got there and made the anonymous 911 call, but he would have been in a hurry to get out of the house before the police showed up so I think he would have ignored it." I looked at her and smiled, "It had to be someone who didn't realize Slinger was dead and was kind enough to pick it up for him."

"Yes, it was me."

"What happened?"

"It was that night, knit night, that I took over the lasagnas I made for him that week. He always left his back door unlocked for me and usually I just put the food in his freezer and left. The less I saw him the better. But that night the door was ajar which was odd, so after I put the food away I called out. He didn't reply but I could see him sitting in his chair with his back to me and his knitting lying on the floor. I didn't think, I just went in and picked it up to hand to him. When I saw him I dropped it and ran. I didn't touch him or anything else I just ran out the back door."

"Minnie, I probably would have done the same thing," I consoled her.

"Maybe but I should have told you and I should have told the police. You're my friend and you were helping me and I convinced myself that I would tell you when the time was right. And of course it never was."

"Oh Minnie, it doesn't matter about me!"

"Yes, it does and I'm truly sorry."

I got up and gave her a quick hug. "You know telling the police this wouldn't have helped to solve the crime so it's not such a big deal. And anyway we both held back something from the police so I'm just as bad as you."

"No, you were a good friend. You didn't tell them about the blackmail because I asked you not to. It's me who kept the secrets and it is me who has to fix this," she said adamantly. "I'm on my way to the police station right now."

"Do you want me to go with you?"

"No, I'll be fine. I just felt you should know first. And I really am sorry I kept it from you and worried you."

She pulled on her coat and I watched her go down the steps, head held high, once again the Minnie I knew and loved.

It wasn't until the next day that Jack phoned to arrange a meeting. I arrived at Beansters before him and got an armchair next to the sunniest corner window.

I splurged on an extra large London Fog and waited for him to arrive. He waved as he came in. He was casually dressed in a denim shirt and jeans with high top runners. He looked relaxed and frankly fabulous. He got a coffee and carried it to the seat next to mine settling into it with a sigh.

"You look like you've just solved a big case and are off duty."

"Yup. A whole day to myself."

"And you're spending it talking about the case. What a shame!" I teased.

"Hey I love talking about my successes, especially with my expert witness."

I blushed burying myself in my tea fog, "So how is Rose?"

"She told us everything. She's hoping that by telling us she can keep the story away from the press and her sister."

"Do you think that will work? I mean there are a lot of sensational details to the crime. The papers must be all over it. "

"Not my area, privately I think she's worrying over her sister for nothing. I think Camellia knows more than she lets on."

"I think so too." We sipped in silence. "You know what? I should have guessed it was Rose days ago."

"How could you?"

"When you told me there were no fingerprints. Remember I said that the killer must have worn gloves but that didn't help because it was winter. I didn't think of rubber gloves."

"So when did it occur to you?"

"Oh not till later, its just that she was a cleaning lady and they all wear rubber gloves," I said vaguely. I didn't want to tell him about my squash experiment and how my own hands slipped on the metal needle until I'd used rubber gloves during the fiasco.

"Did you know Minnie was involved, that she was at the murder scene?"

I avoided his eyes, answering indirectly, "She only told me yesterday, just before she headed to the station. Are you going to charge her?"

"With what? Obstruction? No, now that we have a confession what would be the point?"

"That's a relief. What about the other blackmail victims?"

"We are still working on it, its pretty complicated. When we interrogated Oscar Richter he told us Slinger was threatening to publicize the lies about the death of Camellia's father."

"What payment did Slinger extract?"

"Besides supplying Slinger with documents which were a potential source of blackmail material, Oscar paid Slinger a couple hundred dollars a month. He called it fees for 'computer servicing.'"

"That's bad but it's not very much."

"No, that was Slinger's genius. Every payment he extracted was small enough that the targets could afford to pay without difficulty. That way they didn't get fed up and the blackmail could go on for years. Like Minnie and her dinners!" he laughed.

"Still its pretty small stuff."

"Ah, but Slinger also had some other scams going too."

"Really? He was busy!"

"And it's keeping us busy too. It helped when Minnie told us about Ken Kim. I've got our tech people working on the possible cell phone scam. But it was when she told us about that mis-directed parcel that we were able to tie the blackmail to Frank's work at the post office. So we brought in Fred Birch, the other manager there. It didn't take much to make him talk." He took a sip of coffee relaxing into the chair. "Slinger and Birch had a sweet deal going. They were overall managers of the place and sifted through the incoming mail and parcels. They were interested in anything sent out from internet shopping sites. Once they saw a pattern of multiple deliveries to one person they watched the mail for that address then lifted the credit card statement for a month or two. "

"Didn't the people notice their bill hadn't arrived?"

"Nope. I'd guess they were hoping if they didn't get a bill they didn't have to pay."

"La La Land!"

"I know. Anyway, with the information from the credit card Frank called pretending to be one of their favorite stores in order to get the cvv code."

"But.." I protested.

Jack grinned, "Yeah, you should never give out your code but to be fair you have to keep in mind that Slinger had a lot of detail about their past purchases from the statements and was probably very polished in his approach."

"Now I know why I'd never be a criminal, I'm just not that smart!"

Jack grinned, "With that information he used the credit card to order gift cards for grocery stores and gas, small stuff like that. But here's the interesting part, we've talked to some of the card owners and they didn't even know they were being cheated."

"I find that hard to believe. How much are you talking about?"

"Say up to a hundred dollars a month."

I thought it over. It was so simple and because it was for such small amounts and over several stores it probably would have gone undetected forever if Slinger hadn't been murdered. I shook my head, "And I suppose it was all Frank's doing?"

"You got it! Poor Fred swears he didn't know what was going on but we found dozens of gift cards in his house. We also found a bunch in Carl Reid's house but he says Slinger gave them to him as a gift."

"How generous of Slinger! I don't suppose you'll be able to prove Reid was in on it?"

"Fred says Carl wanted to take over when Frank died and continue the scam."

"That explains the argument they had in the coffee shop. How did Reid find out about the scamming in the first place?"

"Don't know, Carl's not talking yet."

There was a pause as I thought about what Jack had told me. Then I remembered, "Did you ever find a will? Who gets the car?"

He grinned, "No, no will. Bob gets everything."

"Bob, in a car like that. It just doesn't get any worse. I wonder if he has any idea of the value."

"He'll probably just sell it. Are you interested in buying it?"

I laughed, "No way!"

Jack took a sip. "I have a question for you," he said sitting forward.

Suddenly I was on alert.
"I was thinking of the knitting questions," he said.

I let out my breath, feeling foolish. "Some expert! Most of my theories about the knitting angle were wrong," I admitted. "Except about the unravelling. I got that right."

Jack laughed, "Frogging, you mean."

"Whatever! The only person who could have done it was Mr. Perfectionist himself, Frank Slinger. What confused me was the placement of the blood under the unravelled bits. I thought it must have been frogged after the killing. Since that meant the killer was also a knitter and the only knitter I knew involved in this was Minnie I just stopped thinking about it.

Then when it was clear that Tom was the one who rearranged the pile I was back to Frank. Not that it matters anyway!" I said ruefully.

The little bell on the coffee shop door rang and I looked up to see Claire. Jack waved to her and turned back to me, "Well Amy, thanks for all your help. I really mean it. Being a knitter did help to solve the crime. I don't think Rose would have confessed if you hadn't set up knit night to unmask her. That was a stroke of genius!"

"I wish I could take credit for that, but you know I can't." I wrapped both hands around my mug, "I do hope it goes easily for Rose, she's had a terrible life. I feel sorry for her."

Claire's takeaway coffee was ready. She brought it over, "Hi Amy," she smiled and turned to Jack, "are you almost ready? We're going to be late."

I must have looked surprised.

She continued, "Sorry, we can't stay. Jack told me the whole story last night. Hard to believe isn't it?"

I nodded. It was hard to believe and I wasn't thinking about the murder. I needed some time, enough that it didn't hurt to see my good friend Claire with a man whose company I enjoyed a little too much. I watched them leave, bickering amicably.

Sighing I wondered if Meg would like some company. Springtime in Paris sounds perfect. I finished my tea and walked slowly home in the rain. THE END

KAL* Epilogue

Claire finished her scarf and hated it! The yarn was a lovely handspun but there was just too little for the kind of drape wrap she wanted. She offered it to the knit group and Tessa grabbed it, twisting and sewing it into a gorgeous cowl. Tessa named it the Twisted Scarf to Cowl. For that pattern or the Picot Edged Dishcloth that Frank was knitting for the homeless go to www.rlbeck.com. With the purchase of this book you will get one free download of either pattern.

*KAL is an acronym for knit-along. KALs were dreamed up by knitters to share the fun of making a pattern with other knitters without having to be in the same room or even the same country. And KALs are mysteries! A pattern that is used for a KAL is distributed section by section. For example, if the KAL is a sweater you might get the sleeves one week and the back another and so on. Like a mystery book each new chapter reveals a bit but it's not until the end that you have the full solution.

71442430R00145

Made in the USA
Lexington, KY
21 November 2017